# The Princess School

## Let Down Your Hair

# The Princess School

If the Shoe Fits

Who's the Fairest?

Let Down Your Hair

# The Princess School

## Let Down Your Hair

Jane B. Mason ~ Sarah Hines Stephens

SCHOLASTIC INC.

New York Toronto London Auckland Sydney
Mexico City New Delhi Hong Kong Buenos Aires

Published by Scholastic Inc.
SCHOLASTIC and associated logos are trademarks
and/or registered trademarks of Scholastic Inc.

ISBN 0-439-62939-X

12 11 10 9 8 7 6 7 8 9/0

Printed in the U.S.A. 40

First printing, April 2004

For Emmett, Elliot, and Oliver,
our knights in shining armor.

—JBM & SHS

## Chapter One
# A Narrow Escape

Rapunzel Arugula swung herself over the gray stone windowsill of her tower. She had done it so many times, she barely had to look to see where her feet went. But today she was moving slower than usual. She'd woken up with a sore neck.

Maybe the weight of Madame Gothel's daily descent from the tower on her braid was getting to her. *Or maybe Princess School is making me soft,* Rapunzel mused as she lowered her leg to the next foothold.

In spite of the ache in her neck, Rapunzel grinned. On her first day of Princess School she had been sure the other students were nothing but silly, frilly girls. Now she knew better. A lot of the girls were interesting and fun. And her friends Snow White, Cinderella, and Briar Rose were the best. They were smart, funny, and always there for her.

Ella, Rose, and Snow weren't Rapunzel's only friends, of course. She and Prince Valerian had been pals for years. But Rapunzel got something different from her girlfriends. They understood how life was. They made her feel, well, like she was a part of something.

Rapunzel grabbed hold of the pointy reddish rock a few feet above the ground. Then with a little kick she swung her body away from the stone wall and jumped to the ground. Another successful descent.

Brushing off her hands, Rapunzel looked up at her small, round tower. It was utterly familiar. She'd lived there for as long as she could remember — ever since Madame Gothel took her from her parents when she was just a baby.

Rapunzel couldn't remember her parents at all. She had no idea what they looked like or who they were. Madame Gothel never mentioned them and Rapunzel didn't ask. She didn't want the old witch to know she cared. She used to daydream about them all the time, imagining what life would be like if they were bringing her up instead of Madame Gothel — if you could call what she was doing "bringing her up." It often felt more like holding her down.

But in the past few months Rapunzel hadn't been thinking about her parents. She had been focusing on other things — on school, on her friends, on the reflective flash code she'd invented to communicate with Val while she was at Princess School and he was at the Charm School for Boys.

Rapunzel leaned against the gnarled trunk of a giant oak. She rubbed her neck and looked around for Val. Where was that prince, anyway? Rapunzel tapped her foot on the ground. Late, as usual.

All of a sudden a dark cloud covered the sun, casting a shadow across the tower. Shivering, Rapunzel pulled her cloak around her shoulders. What was going on? She stood perfectly still and listened. All was silent — even the birds had stopped singing.

Rapunzel's heart beat quickly. Only one thing silenced the birds.

Charging the tower and ignoring her stiff neck, Rapunzel leaped as high as she could and began to climb. Her hands and feet found their regular holds as she vaulted her body upward. A moment later she hurled her leg over the windowsill and threw herself onto her lumpy bed. She barely had time for a single breath before Madame Gothel appeared in her room in a puff of greenish smoke.

"Lizard's leg!" she screeched. "How can I search for good potion roots without my basket?" Her steely gray eyes glinted at Rapunzel, looking her over carefully. Pretending to stretch, Rapunzel quickly tucked her feet under the skirt of her gown. She didn't want the witch to spot her muddy shoes. She let out what she hoped was a convincing yawn.

"Now where is that basket?" Madame Gothel looked toward a small side table where the basket lay on its side. But Rapunzel was already on her feet, reaching for the willow container.

"It's right here!" Rapunzel held it toward the witch and did her best to keep her breath even.

*I can't believe I didn't notice it was here,* she scolded herself. *What if she had come sooner?* Madame Gothel's visits were almost always predictable. She appeared in the tower twice a day — once to deliver breakfast and again to deliver supper. She always arrived in a green cloud and always departed out the tower window using Rapunzel's braid as a rope. And she never left anything behind without Rapunzel noticing. At least not until now.

"I see it," Madame Gothel snapped, snatching the basket. "I'm not blind."

Rapunzel shuddered. That was what she was afraid of. If Madame Gothel had come a moment earlier, she would have been caught for sure. Madame Gothel had no idea Rapunzel was going to Princess School. And if she found out, Rapunzel wouldn't be able to go any longer. As it was, the witch seemed slightly suspicious. Her gaze fell repeatedly to the bottom of Rapunzel's gown. Rapunzel felt sure she was trying to get another look at her shoes. And she seemed in no hurry to leave, which was unusual. She didn't normally linger in the tower.

Rapunzel uncoiled her braid and made her way to the tower window. She couldn't remember the last time she'd felt so nervous. And not just for herself. "I can lower you whenever you are ready," she said loudly. She quickly stole a glance at the oak tree and the path below.

*Please let Val be hiding behind that tree,* she thought. *Or be even later than usual!*

## Chapter Two
# Through the Woods

Leaping over a fallen tree trunk, Rapunzel grabbed her l-o-n-g braid and slung it over her shoulder for the third time. It kept falling out and was driving her crazy. But there had been no time to re-coil it.

Madame Gothel had lingered in her room for what seemed like ages, describing in great detail the cackle syrup and wart-growing potions she'd been concocting. She'd gone on so long Rapunzel and Val would be lucky if they made it to school on time.

"I think she might suspect something!" Rapunzel shouted as she pushed aside a wayward branch.

Val was right behind her. "Don't worry," he said, panting. "You've been getting out of that tower for years and she's never even guessed. You're probably imagining it."

"I know," Rapunzel groaned. "But if she ever finds out I've started going to Princess School . . ." She swallowed hard. Princess School was the best thing to happen to her, well, *ever.* She couldn't possibly give it up now!

Val's green eyes looked serious. "Well, maybe you should be more careful," he advised.

Just then the sparkling towers of the giant castle school came into view. It was a beautiful sight, one Rapunzel would sorely miss if her witch caretaker found out what she was up to.

"See you after school!" Rapunzel called. She lifted her skirts higher and charged across the Princess School bridge, startling the swans in the moat. She bounded up the steps, two at a time, and the doors whooshed open as she approached. Rapunzel loved that. It made her feel royal.

Clusters of princesses lingered in the hall, chatting. A group of fourth-year Crowns was laughing lightly over a shared joke. Several third-year Robes were gossiping about a boy from the Charm School. Some second-year Sashes marveled over a classmate's new dress. Rapunzel scanned a group of first-year Bloomers as she let out a sigh of relief. Obviously the final trumpet had not yet sounded. Rapunzel slowed to a walk and quickly tried to make a proper bun with her ropy hair. It wasn't easy, but she'd learned a lot in Looking Glass class and from Rose, who really knew her way around a head of hair — even an unwieldy one like Rapunzel's.

"Rapunzel!" called a voice from up ahead. It was Ella. Snow and Rose were with her. "We were beginning to worry about you. You know how rigid Madame Garabaldi is now that exams are coming up!"

Rapunzel rolled her eyes. "Madame Garabaldi is nothing compared to what I had to deal with this morning. Madame Gothel showed up just as I was leaving," she explained. "I barely got back in my tower before she appeared!"

Snow shivered. "I can't believe she silences the birds," she said. "The poor little things!"

Rapunzel waved a hand through the air. "The birds are fine," she said. "But I'm a little worried that Madame Gothel knows I'm getting out. She's never paid me extra visits before." Her breath caught in her throat. "If she figures it out, I . . . I . . ."

"She won't," Rose said firmly. Her lovely blue eyes looked determined as she tucked a stray lock of hair behind Rapunzel's ear and smiled reassuringly.

Ella linked an arm through Rapunzel's. "We've got to get to hearthroom," she said. "And after that we're off to our first class in Cordial Correspondence! We're going to be paired with boys from the Charm School. I can't wait!"

Rose and Snow both giggled, and Rapunzel rolled her eyes again. But truth be told, she had been looking forward to Cordial Correspondence class, too. It sounded much more fun than all the girly things they had to do in Looking Glass, and less impossible than Stitchery. It would be nice to start something completely new — especially if she could figure out how to be paired with Val. Their light-flashing code was great, but there was only so much you could say with light and mirrors. Letters would be a lot more detailed — and fun.

The final trumpet blasted, echoing off the alabaster walls and carved arches. Ella, Snow, Rose, and Rapunzel hurried down the hall together, their slippered feet padding softly on the pink-and-white marble floor. They made it through their hearthroom door and into their high-backed, velvet-cushioned seats seconds before Madame Garabaldi strode into the room.

Rapunzel stopped rubbing her neck and sat up a little straighter. Madame Garabaldi had a way of making you do that.

"Good morning, princesses," the teacher said briskly. She picked up a large parchment, unrolled it, and immediately began scroll call. She rapped out names like a king commanding troops, looking up over her half-spectacles as each girl replied. When she was finished, she set the scroll down and began to pace back and forth across the front of the room.

"Beginning next week you will all be alloted time to study during hearthroom in recognition of the more vigorous academic schedule you must follow to prepare for the impending exams," Madame Garabaldi announced. "They are closer than you think. You will also begin a new unit today: Cordial Correspondence. You will improve your pen-princessship. You will refine your royal language skills. In short, you will begin to learn how to communicate regally." Madame Garabaldi raised her sharp nose into the air slightly. "I hope all of you will take this new unit seriously. I do not want to find myself disappointed in any of you. And it is not an excuse to neglect your extra exam studies." She gazed at several of the princesses in turn, finishing with Rapunzel.

Rapunzel bristled. She knew she was not as princessy as the rest of her classmates. And she didn't always take her classes seriously (it was hard to think of Stitchery as a serious subject!). As Madame Garabaldi stared, Rapunzel shifted in her seat. Something in the teacher's eyes made Rapunzel feel suddenly nervous, as if Madame Garabaldi could see right through her. She wondered if Madame Garabaldi knew what made Rapunzel different. Maybe Madame Garabaldi could tell that Rapunzel had been raised by a witch.

Lost in thought, Rapunzel jumped when the end-of-class trumpet sounded. She followed as the princesses spilled into the hall, stopping at their velvet-lined trunks to get their materials for Cordial Correspondence. Rapunzel joined her friends at Ella's trunk.

Rose held up a beautiful rose stamp she had brought to seal her scrolls. "My parents just gave it to me," she explained.

Snow had some old scrolls her mother had written to her father during their courtship. "My stepmother ordered a servant to destroy them, but he gave them to me instead," she whispered, her eyes wide.

Even Ella had a lovely silver calligraphy pen. "It was my mother's," she said with a glowing smile. "My stepmother doesn't know my dad gave it to me."

Rapunzel bit her lip. She hadn't brought anything for her new class. As the girls made their way to the Cordial Correspondence classroom on the top floor of the castle, her friends chattered excitedly. Rapunzel was silent.

"My goodness," Snow said breathlessly, stepping into the class chamber.

"It practically glitters!" Ella said, looking around the room. Light poured into the room through the diamond-paned, floor-to-ceiling windows. Silver platters lined with seals and colorful candles sat next to stacks of pastel-colored parchment on polished marble tables.

Rapunzel sat down at a carved wooden desk. An inkwell and a pen with a fluffy pink feather sat before her.

Just then their teacher, Sir Spondence, ambled into the room. Rapunzel grinned as soon as she saw him. His thinning silver hair was perfectly groomed, as was his wide, curved mustache and pointed goatee. He wore puffy short pantaloons with stockings and a short waistcoat with tails — neatly tailored and starched. They suited him perfectly.

"Potential royals," he said warmly. "My first order of business is to communicate to you the name of the young prince with whom each of you will correspond for the duration of the course." He unrolled a large, cream-colored scroll.

Rapunzel crossed her fingers under her desk. *Please let me get Val,* she thought. *Please, please, please!*

"Snow White will have the privilege of corresponding with Hans Charming," Sir Spondence announced. Snow giggled, her pale face turning slightly pink. "Scarlet Riding Hood shall be paired with Hector Velveteen. Cinderella Brown shall exchange pleasantries with Allister Arlington."

"The best dancer from the Charm School," Rose whispered. This time it was Ella's turn to blush.

Rapunzel was already working on a new secret code to use in her letters to Val.

"Briar Rose will be expressing her royal thoughts to Valentine Valerian."

Rapunzel looked up. What was that?

"And Rapunzel Arugula shall correspond with Oliver Eggert," Sir Spondence finished.

Rapunzel's jaw dropped.

As Sir Spondence lowered the scroll, murmurs echoed through the room.

"Hans Charming!" Snow said with an excited giggle. The Charming boys were famous throughout the kingdom for their good looks and fine manners.

"I get to write to Val!" Rose said. Her always-pink cheeks looked a little extra flushed.

Rapunzel scowled. She did not want to write to Oliver Eggert. And even worse, she didn't want Rose to write to Val! He always acted so goofy about Rose. All of the boys did, and most of the girls. It drove Rapunzel crazy the way people fawned over Rose and called her "Beauty."

"Kindly make your way to the front of the room and choose an unsullied paper," Sir Spondence instructed. "Today you shall be writing a simple letter of introduction."

Rapunzel felt as though she were weighted to her desk. First Madame Gothel practically catches her outside her tower, and now this! She watched as the other girls chose parchments and returned to their seats. Stifling a groan, she did the same.

Rapunzel watched Ella dip her mother's silver pen in the inkwell and begin to write. Snow's old scrolls lay on her desk next to the paper she was writing on. And Rose's stamp was ready to be used for the first time.

Rapunzel had a knot in her stomach. Her friends had all brought something special — a piece of home, of family . . . the one thing Rapunzel didn't have.

Gazing out the window, Rapunzel let her mind wander. What *would* it be like to have a family? To be surrounded by people who loved her all the time, like the way the dwarves doted on Snow, or how Rose was adored by . . . well . . . everyone. Rapunzel was grateful for her friends, but families were different. More permanent.

*I don't even know when my birthday is,* Rapunzel thought miserably. *Or what my mother looked like. Or if she would even like me.*

Without thinking, Rapunzel picked up her pen, dipped it in the inkwell, and began to write. But she wasn't writing to Oliver Eggert. Or Val. She was writing to her mother.

*Dear Mother,*

*I know it is strange, me writing to you. But so many things seem strange to me lately. I feel as though my whole world is changing before my eyes, and I can only watch. I love Princess School and my new friends. For the first time I feel connected to something. But sometimes I feel so different from everyone else. My friends all seem to have things that I don't. We are taking a new class called Cordial Correspondence, and I had hoped to be able to write to my good friend Prince Val. You'd like him. But my friend Briar Rose will be writing to him instead. It just doesn't seem fair. I need Val right now. He knows me better than anyone. But now he'll be busy writing to Rose. I wish you were here, Mother. Then I would have someone to talk to.*

*Love,*
*Your Daughter, Rapunzel*

## Chapter Three
# Cordial Creations

Ella dipped her silver pen into the inkwell and paused to examine her letter. So far she had introduced herself and thanked Allister for their dances at the Coronation Ball.

She ran her finger lightly over the thick paper. It was lovely. And the personalized seals and colorful waxes they'd use to seal their communications were enough to make any letter seem regal.

Sir Spondence cleared his throat. "In this class you shall compose communication masterpieces so lovely that their recipients will keep them tucked inside the pockets of their royal waistcoats."

Ella and several other girls giggled. A look of surprise from Sir Spondence silenced them, but he soon broke into a grin. Ella smiled back at him. Cordial Correspondence was turning out to be as wonderful as she had hoped. And thanks to her mother's lessons years ago, her calligraphy wasn't too embarrassing.

Ella gazed around the room. Most of the princesses were writing busily, but Rapunzel was staring out the window, seemingly lost in thought. Her paper was partially filled. Ella tried to catch her friend's eye, but Rapunzel looked over at Rose, who was bent low over her paper. The quill in Rose's hand danced over her paper, and she was smiling broadly. Rapunzel glowered.

"Sir Spondence," asked Ariel, a petite princess with flowing red hair. "How will we send our correspondences once they are written?"

"Hear this, clever students," Sir Spondence replied. He tugged at his waistcoat and lowered his voice, as if he were about to tell them a great secret. "Composing the correspondence is but the beginning of a letter's grand journey. Once completed and sealed, your perfect post must find its way to its intended recipient via one of three royal methods: wing, willow, or woodland creature."

The teacher straightened and opened a window. A gust of wind blew into the room, ruffling his perfectly coiffed hair. "Though the breeze is brisk," he said, "I am inclined to advise that today we should send by . . . willow! You shall each have an additional turn of the time-glass to complete your missives. Then, after the initial sealing ceremony, we shall venture forth together to the enchanted postal tree."

Only one turn of the glass! Ella looked down at her note. There must be something more to say — she just wasn't sure what. After rejecting several ideas she simply wrote: "I am very much looking forward to communicating with you. Your Royal Friend, Cinderella Brown."

"And now for the seals!" Sir Spondence crowed. "Each of you may come forward and select a seal. Choose carefully, for your seal is the mark you will leave on each and every epistle you send forth this term."

All at once the princesses leaped from their seats and rushed to the front of the room. By the time Ella reached the marble table, several girls had already made their seal selections. Rose had her rose, of course. Snow was exclaiming with delight over a tiny hummingbird. Rapunzel had a tight grip on a seal with a knot impressed in it. Ella looked through the remaining seals. There was a daffodil, a perfectly tied bow, a unicorn, a crown . . . all lovely, but none of them just right.

"What about this one?" Snow asked, holding up a seal. "It's perfect for you!"

Ella leaned closer and her eyes widened. It was a slipper!

Snow slid the seal into Ella's hand. The silvery

metal was cool to the touch, and the weight of it took Ella by surprise. It was heavier than she thought it would be. But Snow was right. It was perfect.

"Ladies, ladies," Sir Spondence said from the sealing table a few feet away. "Gather 'round and I shall demonstrate the art of sealing a royal missive."

The teacher stood before a large marble table. A polished silver tray sat in the middle, heaped with candles of every imaginable color. Behind the tray was a single white taper, already burning.

Sir Spondence chose a dark blue sealing candle and lit it using the white taper. Ella held her breath as, carefully holding the blue candle over the thick parchment, he allowed several drops of melted wax to fall onto the rolled paper.

Sir Spondence let seven drops fall, then quickly blew out the blue candle. Placing his feathery quill seal over the hot wax, he pressed firmly but gently, uniting the two ends of parchment.

"Voilà!" he said, blowing lightly on the wax to help it harden. "A perfectly cordial, perfectly sealed correspondence. And now, ladies, it is your turn."

The girls excitedly chose their colors and began to practice their sealing.

"Ooops!" Snow cried as she dripped a few too many drops of yellow wax on her parchment. She pressed her hummingbird seal onto the warm liquid. "Poor thing! He looks like he's stuck in a mud puddle!" she giggled.

Next to Snow, Gretel's wax was falling onto the white marble table.

"Here," Rapunzel said, handing her a lace cloth to wipe it up.

"Wow, Rose," Ella said admiringly. "Your rose looks perfect."

"It does," Snow chirped.

"Thanks," Rose said.

Next to Ella, Rapunzel pressed her knot seal hard onto her melted wax. And, Ella noticed, she was frowning again.

Clutching their letters so they wouldn't blow away, the princesses followed Sir Spondence to the postal tree.

"I must say this breeze is unseasonably brisk," the instructor said over the howling wind. "But we shall not be deterred in our delivery!"

He led the way to the huge, gnarled willow that sat on the edge of the Princess School grounds.

"It doesn't look enchanted to me," Snow whispered as they approached the tree.

"Each of you may slip your missive into the knothole," he said.

Ella stepped forward eagerly and dropped her rolled parchment into the tree. She moved aside to make room for Snow, who gave the tree a funny little curtsy before slipping her roll through the hole. She was giving the trunk a thank-you pat when Rose placed her correspondence in the hole in a single, graceful motion. The other Bloomers sent off their scrolls, too. Only Rapunzel, Ella noticed, seemed to hesitate. She clutched her letter to her chest and remained several feet away from the tree.

"Rapunzel," Ella said, approaching her friend. "It's your turn."

Rapunzel's eyes were full of uncertainty. Ella was about to say something encouraging when the willow suddenly snaked a tendril over Rapunzel's shoulder and snatched the letter. A moment later the giant tree stuffed the scroll into its knothole as if feeding a hungry mouth.

Rapunzel stared up at the tree, horrified.

"Mr. Willow!" Snow scolded. "How terribly rude!" She strode over to Rapunzel and placed a comforting hand on her friend's shoulder.

"Are you all right?" Rose asked.

Rapunzel's eyes flashed. "I'm fine," she snapped.

Ella was taken aback by Rapunzel's harsh reply. Rose was only being nice.

The knothole was now sealed, and the tree's branches blew carelessly about, as if mocking the girls.

"Don't worry, Rapunzel," Ella said. "I'm sure your letter will be delivered just fine."

*She must be upset about her near run-in with Madame Gothel,* Ella thought. She turned to their instructor. "How *do* the letters get delivered, Sir Spondence?" she asked, hoping for an explanation that would console her friend. Rapunzel was usually so unflappable, but she seemed pretty shaken. And it was just a scroll.

Sir Spondence looked a little perplexed by the question and paused before he began to speak. "Ah, the delivery of royal missives is, um, a long-lived tradition. Each letter must . . . ah . . . travel the distance, short or vast, reaching its destination only when the passage has been successfully navigated," he finally replied.

While Snow nodded eagerly, Ella gave Rose a confused look. *What was that supposed to mean?*

"Eventually, the letters will reach the Charmed Cherry, the ancient fruit tree at the edge of the Charm School grounds," Sir Spondence finished somewhat meekly.

Just then a cold gust of wind caught the group by surprise, and Sir Spondence stumbled. Frowning slightly, he looked up at the sky. "All's well!" Sir Spondence clapped his hands together. "Back to class, my ladies," he said in his cheerful voice. But his eyes registered concern, and Ella saw Rapunzel turn back to the tree, glaring fiercely.

All was not well.

# Chapter Four
# Blowup

Rapunzel kicked a stone along the path while she waited for Val to catch up. He could be such a slowpoke! But she wasn't really annoyed about having to wait for him. She was used to that. She was annoyed about the willow tree stealing her letter.

"That dumb tree stole my personal thoughts right out of my hand!" she said to a squirrel munching on an acorn nearby. His fur was standing on end from the gusty wind that had been blowing hard all day. "And then it ate them!" This wasn't entirely true, of course. The willow had actually stuffed the letter into its mail slot so that it could be delivered to the proper place. But that was just the problem. Since the letter was to Rapunzel's mother, there *was* no proper place.

Rapunzel wasn't exactly sure why she had written the letter. She knew her mother would never get it. But writing out all her thoughts and feelings had felt pretty good.

Until that nasty willow stole it away. Now her letter could end up anywhere! What if her innermost thoughts wound up in the hands of some Charm School boy — or, worse, a witch at the Grimm School!

Rapunzel pictured Hortense Hegbottom cackling madly as she read all about how Rapunzel missed her mother. Ugh! What a nightmare!

Shifting her book satchel and picking up a rock, she threw it as hard as she could into the stream that ran next to the path. But the wind tossed it farther than she'd intended, and it bounced off a tree on the other side of the brook.

"Nice throw," called out a voice. It was Val. He ran up and stopped right in front of her to catch his breath. Rapunzel was grateful to see a friendly face. She was about to tell him everything that had happened when Val started in about the Charm School's Correspondence course.

"I thought it would be totally boring," he admitted as he started down the path. "I mean, what's interesting about writing letters? But having Rose for a correspondent is going to be great! I'm sure her pen-princessship is terrific. And the other princes are all jealous I got Beauty."

Rapunzel's jaw dropped. Was he kidding? Since when did Val give a crown about pen-princessship? She felt a surge of jealousy. He didn't care about calligraphy. What he cared about was Rose.

"Did you have to do your introductory notes today?" Val asked.

"Of course. That's how you always begin the class," Rapunzel replied flatly, like she was an expert.

"Professor Insignia told us we'll be writing our introductions tomorrow. But he seemed surprised when your letters hadn't arrived in time for our afternoon class."

"How fascinating," Rapunzel said sarcastically. Val didn't seem to notice.

A gust of wind stirred up a layer of dust on the path, and Rapunzel shielded her eyes. What was with the weather? It had been so weird today.

"What a wind," Val said, echoing Rapunzel's thoughts.

"Uh-huh," Rapunzel replied dully. She did not want to encourage him to go on about anything. Especially Correspondence and Rose.

Val looked back at Rapunzel. Confusion showed in his eyes. Lowering his head, he hurried up the path in silence.

Rapunzel sighed. She hadn't meant to be mean. It wasn't Val's fault he'd been paired with Rose. But couldn't he have said he'd have liked to have been paired with Rapunzel just as much? That it would be great for them to correspond, too?

The wind unraveled a few strands of Rapunzel's braid and they flew across her face. Halfheartedly she tucked them back in and followed several paces behind her friend. She wished her girlfriends were there. They would listen to her. They would understand her worries about her letter.

When their paths split off, Val waved good-bye but didn't call out. The wind was howling now, and Rapunzel knew she probably would not have heard him anyway. But she also knew that wasn't why he was silent, and a fresh wave of guilt washed over her as she watched him walk away. She shook her head and began to climb the tower, grabbing hold of the familiar stones and cracks. A few minutes later she hoisted herself over the windowsill. Glad to get out of the wind, she was about to shutter the window when she heard something behind her.

"Newt's nostrils!" shrieked an angry voice.

Rapunzel whirled around. Madame Gothel stood in the middle of her tower room, her gnarled hands balled into fists.

"I see you have been deceiving me, Rapunzel," she hissed. "Escaping the protective haven I've so carefully created for you." She eyed Rapunzel's heavy satchel.

"And going to . . . to . . . Princess School!" She spat out "Princess School" as if it were rancid cheese. Then she stepped forward, her gray eyes as sharp as daggers. "But I swear on my best possum potion, you are not a princess. You are the abandoned daughter of poor, *thieving* parents!"

Rapunzel stepped forward, her face hot with fury. "I was not abandoned. And my parents aren't thieves! I was stolen — by you, you evil witch!"

"Stolen?" Madame Gothel screeched. "Stolen? Snake's spit! I granted your parents their fondest wish. How many times I heard your mother cooing in your ear when you were a babe — every night, always the same wish."

The old witch picked up Rapunzel's lumpy pillow and rocked it like a baby. "'Please, keep this child safe,'" she said in a sickeningly beseeching voice. "'Don't let the world harm a single hair on her beautiful head.'"

Madame Gothel dropped the pillow onto the bed like a soiled diaper. "And, by my wart, that is exactly what I have done."

Rapunzel longed to lunge forward and scratch out the old woman's eyes. But she knew better than to try. Madame Gothel was crafty, and she knew a lot of icky spells.

"You haven't kept me safe," she said, forcing her

hands to be still at her sides. "You've kept me imprisoned."

"Safe," Madame Gothel hissed.

Rapunzel stepped so close to the witch that their noses almost touched. "Imprisoned," Rapunzel said.

The two stood nose to nose for several seconds. Outside, the wind howled around the tower. Then Madame Gothel stepped back. "You shall not escape your tower again," she announced, her eyes glinting. "Now, lower your hair and let me out of here."

Anger still burned in Rapunzel like a bonfire, but she knew she had no choice but to obey. Uncoiling her hair, she allowed Madame Gothel to lower herself to the ground. Then she threw herself onto her straw mattress and squeezed her eyes shut to hold back a torrent of unspilled tears.

# Chapter Five
# Thick as Pea Soup

Snow tugged the last wrinkle out of the cover on Dim's tiny bed and gave the pillow a pat. "There!" she said, satisfied. The dwarves had already left for the mines, but Snow didn't like to go before the house was tidied up. It was so much cheerier to come home to a clean house.

Grabbing her cloak, Snow dashed downstairs. It was still early. She knew she should probably spend the extra time studying, but decided to meet Rapunzel and Val so they could all walk to school together instead. After all, the exams were still weeks away. Looking over her shoulder, Snow smiled at her cozy cottage and waved good-bye. It didn't matter that nobody was there. Snow felt sure some of the field mice and birds were watching her depart.

Skipping blithely down the path, Snow slowed down when she got to the dogwood tree where the path branched. She glanced at the three arrow-shaped signs on the trunk. A fine mist swirled around the tree, making the signs hard to read. But Snow knew what they said. The arrow that pointed right read TOWN. The arrow that pointed left read GRANDMA'S HOUSE. And the arrow that pointed the way Snow had come read ENCHANTED FOREST.

Snow took the path toward Grandma's House. It was also the way to Rapunzel's tower, but her home was supposed to be a secret. Only Rapunzel, her friends, and the witch who locked up Rapunzel knew how to find it.

As she bounced toward the tower, the mist grew thicker around Snow's feet, hiding the trail. She stopped skipping and felt her way slowly along the path in her thin slippers.

"Oh, my," Snow said softly as the fog grew even more dense. "It's as thick as pea soup!" she chirped to nobody in particular.

Though Snow sounded like her cheerful self, the fog was making her feel unsettled. Turning, she looked back the way she had come. She couldn't see a thing! The fog blanketed her path completely.

"Oh, my, my!" Snow said again. Then she began to hum. Humming almost always made her feel better. When it didn't work, she pursed her lips and whistled, practicing her best birdsongs — but not even the finch's chipper song was helping. Snow felt as though the fog were seeping into her. She was lost and damp and frightened. Panic rose in her chest. She opened her mouth to sing and —

"Oh!" Snow stumbled on a fuzzy rock in the path and pitched forward onto a mossy bank. What was that? Snow reached out to clear the rock from the path and pulled her hand back in alarm. It moved! It was warm and soft, too. Snow stretched her hand out again.

"Why, you're not a rock at all!" Snow picked up a rabbit and held it close to her face. Two more rabbits jumped into her lap. "Bunnies! Have you come to rescue me?" Snow asked. She felt better already. "What darlings!"

While Snow rubbed noses with the rock rabbit, a sparrow sailed through the low-lying cloud, landed on her shoulder, and whistled softly.

"I feel ever so much better now that you're here," Snow told the animals.

She stroked the bunnies and whistled with the sparrow. Suddenly a crash in the thicket startled Snow and the animals. They turned as a young buck with tiny nubs for antlers stepped up next to them. He nuzzled Snow's elbow, and she leaned on him to stand back up. "Oh, what a deer!" Snow giggled.

Surrounded by her woodland friends, Snow felt

more confident. They were all a bit jumpy, and the fog still swirled around them, but they made their way down the path together. Snow followed the white tail of the young deer ahead of her, while the bunnies darted around her feet and the sparrow crooned his sweet song on her shoulder. Now and again, Snow thought she heard something else, too. Familiar voices — Val! And Rapunzel!

"We must be close!" Snow told the animals. The buck walked onward and soon, though she could not see it, Snow sensed that they were in the clearing around the tower.

"Rapunzel!" Snow called.

"Snow? Is that you?" a voice replied from the whiteness above her head. "I can't see to climb down. And I think Val is lost!"

"You can do it, Rapunzel. I just know you can," Snow called up encouragingly. "You've been doing it for years." The first time Snow had watched Rapunzel scale down her tower, her jaw had dropped. She had climbed the wall like a lizard!

"I feel dizzy. I can't see my feet," Rapunzel shouted. The fog was so thick it even muffled her voice, but Snow could still hear her friend's worry.

"You don't need to see your feet. Just close your eyes and follow the sound of my voice." Snow began to sing a simple song the dwarves had taught her. It did the trick. A moment later, Rapunzel was standing at her side.

"Thanks!" Rapunzel said. She spoke softly now and leaned in close to see Snow's face. "We had better get out of here quickly. And we'd better find Val before he wanders into the swamp — or worse!"

Rapunzel walked quickly even in the fog. And she seemed sort of . . . nervous. *It's probably just the fog,* Snow thought. *Or the blind descent she just made.*

"The deer knows the way," Snow said. She hoped her words would be reassuring.

"I know the way," Rapunzel replied a little shortly. "I mean, I've been on this path a zillion times before. It's just —"

Rapunzel was interrupted by the sound of rustling leaves and breaking branches.

"By my sword!" a voice cried just off the path to the left. "Yowch!"

Val.

"Over here, your highness." Rapunzel held out a hand and pulled a rather bedraggled prince onto the path. Val had a branch wrapped in his dark curls and a leaf sticking out of his vest. He was rubbing his forehead.

"Um, hi," he said, smiling. "I guess I sort of lost my way."

"It's the fog," Snow said.

"But I found this!" Val pulled the thorny branch out of his hair and offered the girls a few berries from it.

"We don't have time for a snack now," Rapunzel said. She was still speaking more softly than usual. "We're late. And Madame Gothel might be looking for me."

"Don't be ridiculous!" Val said, popping a berry in his mouth. "Why would Madame Gothel look for you?" Val teased. "You're always right where she left you."

"Listen. She knows I get out," Rapunzel said gravely. "She saw me yesterday. And if she catches me doing it again I don't know what she'll do." She paused and took a deep breath. "This could be my last day of freedom."

Snow gasped. This was terrible news! She couldn't imagine Princess School without Rapunzel! Snow's mind spun with questions and worries. How did the witch find out? What had she said to Rapunzel? And most important, what were they going to do now? Beside her, Val was speechless. And Rapunzel was already marching down the path toward school.

## Chapter Six

# Signed, Sealed . . . Delivered?

Rose shifted in her seat, waiting for Sir Spondence to speak. Instead the instructor peered out the tall classroom windows and gave his well-trimmed goatee three quick tugs. His swooping eyebrows sat low over his eyes as he looked into the fog.

"Alas, my ladies. In all the days it has been my pleasure to instruct fine, unformed royals in the art of courtly communication" — he paused dramatically — "I have never waited such a prolonged period to receive a return communiqué. I cannot believe that the Charm School has lost its charm. No, I simply cannot."

"Neither can I," Snow whispered to Rose. "Hans Charming is just, well, too charming!"

Not hearing her, Sir Spondence sank into his well-upholstered chair and looked with worry at the girls sitting expectantly before him, each at her own carved writing desk. "I greatly fear something is awry," he confessed. Then he sat up straighter, as if pulling strength from a hidden inner wellspring. "Yet, we shall not be deterred! We need not a missive in hand to compose another!"

Rose couldn't hide the small smile that played on her lips. Sir Spondence was *so* serious. He spoke as if he were trying to inspire an army to battle, not a group of princesses to write! She picked up her quill, gently wiping the tip on the inkwell so it would not drip on the thick parchment.

*My Dear Prince Valerian,* Rose began. Suddenly she felt something tap her knee. Snow was handing back a small scroll under the desk without turning around. Rose carefully took the scroll in her left hand without moving her quill from the paper. If Snow was passing scrolls, it must be important. Scroll-passing was seriously frowned upon in Princess School. Royals used pages and courtly communications — not notes on scraps — to convey their messages. Rose unrolled the tiny parchment in her lap and read:

*We need to talk about Rapunzel's tower trouble. Soon!*

Rose glanced at Rapunzel. She was hunched over her scroll, dripping ink onto her desk, parchment, and sleeve. She didn't look like she was in trouble. She just looked like Rapunzel — feisty and independent, with no princess pomp. It seemed to Rose that Rapunzel always had it together. And she didn't have any meddling parents to deal with or spying fairies "looking out for her," like Rose had. And even if she did, Rapunzel probably wouldn't care. That girl could handle anything!

Rose glanced down at the scroll on her lap. She knew Rapunzel was worried that Madame Gothel would find out about Princess School. But since Rapunzel had made it to school, Rose assumed the secret must still be safe.

Still wondering what exactly the trouble could be, Rose continued her letter to Val. Maybe she would ask him what was going on with Rapunzel. He certainly knew her well enough. But who knew if he would ever even get her letter, or if she would get a reply. She decided against it.

While the girls signed and sealed their notes, Sir Spondence peered through the diamond-shaped panes of glass. He pushed open the window just as Rose pressed her seal into the melted wax.

After licking his index finger, Sir Spondence poked it outside. A moment later he pulled it back in with a shiver. He banged the window shut and whirled to face the class. "Whether the weather will cooperate or not, we shall endeavor to deliver our impressive epistles!" he declared, pounding a fist into his open hand. "If it please Your Princesses, the latest letters will be sent by the most courteous of couriers — the woodland creatures!"

*That will cheer up Snow at least,* Rose thought. Snow White loved animals more than anything.

Rose followed Ella and Rapunzel out into the hall and down several flights of stairs. The princesses spoke of exams and correspondence and Charm School boys in hushed voices as they wound their way past ivy- and rose-carved pillars and arches. When the doors to the school whooshed open, Rose shivered. The misty air was cool and they hadn't stopped to get their cloaks. Crossing the garden, Rose leaned over to whisper to Ella. "What's going on?" she asked. Rapunzel was walking up ahead.

Ella shrugged and showed Rose the tiny scroll in her palm. She'd gotten a note, too.

On the other side of the misty garden, Sir Spondence held up his hand. The princesses stopped and gathered around him, huddling close to hear and to keep one another warm.

Sir Spondence pulled a tiny silver whistle from his waistcoat and blew a quick tune. The whistle sounded surprisingly like Snow's whistle — the one she used to call the animals and birds when she scattered seeds and nuts at her cottage. Rose looked at Snow, smiling, to see if she noticed, too. But Snow — who would normally have been dancing a jig at the chance to combine her two loves, school and animals — looked worried.

Breaking out of the circle, Rose started toward her long-haired friend. She simply had to find out what was going on.

She stopped in her tracks when something caught her eye — a figure in a dark cape and striped stockings disappearing into the woods. Rose couldn't be certain, but it looked like a Grimm School witch. And it looked as though the witch was carrying a pink scroll! Rose was about to call out when Sir Spondence shrieked shrilly. The animals had arrived.

A raccoon with ruffled fur staggered close to the girls. He looked tired and wet. The dark circles around his eyes were extra dark, but his eyes were open startlingly wide. A moist badger, three wet foxes, and a shivering warren of sopping rabbits followed the raccoon.

"Whatever is wrong?" Snow asked. She dropped to her knees and began to dry the creatures with her skirts, singing softly to them. A few of the other princesses awkwardly followed suit.

Clearly flustered by the disheveled and shivering animals, Sir Spondence wrung his hands in a most unroyal manner. Rose thought someone should comfort him, too.

"Never," he said, "never have I seen such disorder, such dampness. The woodland creatures look deeply distraught!"

Rose was thinking the exact same thing about Sir Spondence. The mist curled his hair and beard, and the worry gave his eyes a wild look. Just when she thought he would not be able to finish the lesson at all, the stocky teacher took a deep breath and steadied himself.

"Before we can go further you must each select a messenger," Sir Spondence said. The teacher gained confidence as he walked among the princesses handing out ribbons. "When you have secured your scroll you must announce to whom the post shall pass. Speak clearly and kindly."

Rose stooped and chose the closest animal, a dazed-looking porcupine. She quickly stuck her scroll onto the creature's prickly back. She wished she could pet it or something, but its whole body was covered in quills.

"Prince Valerian," she said softly, forcing herself to smile into the animal's face. "Please take this scroll to Prince Valentine Valerian."

The porcupine stared at her blankly. He didn't look like he'd understood a word. Rose wished she had Snow's way with animals, and even thought of asking

Snow for help. But the porcupine, whether it understood or not, had turned and was waddling back into the woods.

Rose watched as the fog swirled around the small creature. The scroll disappeared first in the white mist. And before the tiny porcupine had gone the length of a pink carpet it had completely disappeared, too.

## Chapter Seven

# Correspondence Chaos

Rapunzel watched as the silver fox carrying her scroll to Oliver Eggert trotted into the woods.

Somehow the fox's departure reminded her of the willow tree gobbling up the letter to her mother.

"Another missive duly swallowed," she said when the fox had disappeared. The missing letters gave her an uneasy feeling. So did the strange misty fog that surrounded Princess School. Rapunzel almost felt as if it were following her.

Brushing away her gloomy thoughts, Rapunzel got to her feet. Suddenly hailstones as big as teacups began to pound down around the girls.

"What in the world?" Rapunzel muttered, looking up. That was a mistake. A quail-egg-sized hailstone landed with a thunk on her forehead.

"Ouch!" Rapunzel scowled and rubbed her head. Compared to the hail, fog seemed pleasant. The chunks were icy and sharp and fell mercilessly from the sky. Bloomers and animals ran in all directions.

"Owie!" cried a princess who had been assailed on the arm. She held the sore spot as she ran toward a large oak tree to take cover.

"My gown!" shouted another, not sure which way to go. "It's been torn!"

"We must make our way back to the castle posthaste!" Sir Spondence called over the din.

Suddenly Snow appeared at Rapunzel's side. Rose and Ella were right behind her.

"Come on," Snow whispered. "We're going to the stables."

"Fine with me," Rapunzel replied. She and the other girls stole away from the chaotic group and made their way through the hail to the grass-roofed structure that housed the school's horses. Ella pulled open the heavy wooden door and the girls ducked inside.

Rapunzel led the way into their favorite empty stall — one that had been painted a washed lavender — and slumped down on a bale of hay. The smell of fresh straw and saddle soap met her nostrils, and she began to feel a little better.

"I have never seen anything like that," Ella said, pulling stray bits of icy hail from her hair. "It was awful!"

Snow nodded gravely. "I just hope they make it to shelter!"

"They will," Rapunzel said. She rubbed her forehead. "The castle is only a little farther than the stables."

Snow turned toward her friend. "I was talking about the animals!" she cried. "I mean, the poor creatures were soaked to the skin when they arrived. And then to have to deliver scrolls in this awful weather. . . . It just doesn't seem fair!"

"The weather *is* awfully strange," Ella said thoughtfully.

"Something is going on," Snow stated. "Something . . . spooky."

Rose sat up straighter. "Oh!" she said. "I'm almost positive I just saw a Grimm girl stealing into the woods with one of our scrolls!"

"Really?" Rapunzel asked. "Who?"

"I'm not sure," Rose admitted. "It was so foggy I couldn't really see."

"Those Grimms are trouble," Ella said.

Snow nodded in agreement. "I know," she said. "But we have something even more important to discuss." Snow's big, dark eyes were serious as she nudged Rapunzel. "Tell them," she encouraged.

Rapunzel let out a big sigh. "It's just that Madame Gothel knows for sure I've been escaping from my tower," she said.

Ella and Rose gasped simultaneously.

"She said that I'm no princess, that my parents were poor thieves. And she vowed not to let me escape again!"

Ella looked thoughtful. "Maybe the fog was Madame Gothel's way of trying to keep you in today," she said.

"That makes sense," Rose admitted.

Snow nodded. "That terrible witch said she's not going to let Rapunzel come to school anymore." Her voice was full of alarm.

"She can't do that. Maybe you ought to write *her* a letter," Rose said angrily. "Though she certainly doesn't deserve anything cordial."

The girls laughed halfheartedly, then fell into a worried silence.

"We have to make sure Rapunzel can keep getting out," Snow said. "Val meets her at the tower every morning, but he can't do it alone. It may take more than one person to foil that bad witch."

Rose and Ella nodded solemnly. They were taking it all so seriously! Rapunzel suddenly felt overwhelmed. She knew the trouble brewing with Madame Gothel was bad, but she could handle it, right? She looked at her shoes.

"Don't worry, Rapunzel," Ella said comfortingly. "We won't let Madame Gothel keep you all to herself.

Princess School just wouldn't be the same without you!"

"I can come tomorrow morning," Rose volunteered. "I'll tell the fairies I have curtsy call in the morning. They'll have no idea that rolling out the pink carpet is really just for special school occasions."

Rapunzel looked at the girls surrounding her. They were the greatest friends anyone could ever want. But their concern was making her feel better *and* worse. Snow's eyes were wide. Ella looked nervous. And Rose had just offered to help in the morning even though it would mean getting up early — something she hated to do. They all seemed genuinely worried.

Rapunzel swallowed hard. Maybe the situation was more dire than she thought.

## Chapter Eight
# Writing on the Wall

Rapunzel walked slowly down the path toward the tower. Val had a last-minute jousting practice, so she was walking home by herself, but Rapunzel didn't mind. She had a lot to think about — the weird stuff going on in Cordial Correspondence, her troubles with Madame Gothel, getting ready for exams, her jealousy about Rose and Val, and the worried looks on her friends' faces as they talked together in the stables.

*It's no big deal,* she told herself. *They're just looking out for me. That's what friends do.* But needing help was not a familiar feeling. And Rose was coming to help her tomorrow. That was okay, except that Rose was coming with Val. And if they couldn't get Rapunzel out they'd be walking to school together, alone!

*Val would probably love that,* Rapunzel thought miserably.

Taking a deep breath, Rapunzel untied her cape

and swung it off her shoulders. The strange weather had cleared. In fact, it had turned into a glorious afternoon. The sky was a deep cerulean blue with a few puffy white clouds. A light breeze was blowing, making the leaves whisper happily on the forest trees.

"Rose probably just wants to see Val," Rapunzel said aloud as she gazed up at the sky. The cloud above her was shaped like a flower. As she watched it pass, a lump grew in her stomach. Rose and Val. She hated the way she felt about their relationship. It wasn't like her to be jealous. They were both her good friends. She was glad they got along. So why did their friendship bother her so much?

Ahead of her the path widened and the tower came into view. Rapunzel stared up at it for a minute. It looked different — straighter, rounder — more welcoming somehow. Seeing it made Rapunzel feel oddly better.

*Stop being such a sad jester*, Rapunzel scolded herself. *Things are never as bad as they seem.*

Whistling a tune she'd learned from Snow, Rapunzel skipped forward and began to climb. A minute later she swung her leg over the edge of her windowsill.

Rapunzel peered around her familiar room. Madame Gothel was nowhere to be seen, but she had left a soufflé of wilted greens and a glass of milk on the small table next to her bed. Rapunzel looked at the food in surprise. Though they appeared to be the same bitter greens Madame Gothel always served, the old witch had never made anything as fancy as a soufflé before — and she'd never brought Rapunzel an afternoon snack.

She'd left Rapunzel something else, too. A letter.

Rapunzel eyed the note warily. It was probably filled with threats and accusations. Madame Gothel must have been furious when she'd brought the soufflé and found that Rapunzel was gone.

*Maybe I can just ignore it,* Rapunzel thought. She felt okay for the first time all day and didn't want to break the spell. But she knew she had to read it. And the longer she waited, the worse it would be.

Bracing herself, Rapunzel picked up the letter. It was written on thick, earthen-colored paper, which was folded and sealed with pea-green wax and stamped in the shape of a cast-iron cauldron.

Sitting down on her bed, Rapunzel broke the seal, unfolded the letter, and began to read.

*Rapunzel,*

*Perfect potions. You have been like a daughter to me these last ten years — filling my cauldron with just the right things. Do not worry your head over changes, young Rapunzel. I will make sure things remain the same forever. Forget about Princess School. You have me. You do not need friends. They will only abandon you in the end — something I will never do.*

*Madame Gothel (Mother)*

Rapunzel stared down at the paper in her hand. There had to be a mistake. She looked at the outside again to make sure it really was for her. The letters of her name were clearly written in Madame Gothel's sharp scrawl.

Why would the old witch write such a letter? Rapunzel read it again, and her mouth dropped open even farther than it had before. This time she read each word carefully . . . including the signature. The last word hit her like a slap in the face. It said *Mother.*

Somehow Madame Gothel had received the letter Rapunzel had written to her mother! Even worse, she thought Rapunzel wrote the letter to *her*!

Filled with fury, Rapunzel leaped to her feet and began to pace the floor. How could Madame Gothel *ever* believe that she thought of her as a mother? What mother kept her daughter locked up in a tower for years on end? And what did Madame Gothel know about friends?

"My friends *are* real!" Rapunzel cried to the empty room. "They would never abandon me!"

Rapunzel glanced at the letter again. She ripped it to shreds and threw the pieces out the window where they scattered in the breeze. But she still felt furious. She had to think of something else to do — something that would make Madame Gothel understand her mistake.

Rapunzel looked over at the small hearth. Since the weather was warm, there was no fire burning. But the blackened stick she used to stoke the fire caught her eye. She could use it like a quill to write a response. Since she'd torn up the only paper in the room she would have to write the response right on the wall.

Rapunzel quickly picked up the stick and began to write.

*MG,*

*That letter was not for you.*
*You are not my mother, and never will be.*
*I am not a bird in a cage.*
*You cannot keep me trapped forever.*
*And you do not know my friends.*
*Unlike you, they would never betray me.*

*R.*

She had to blacken the end of the stick in the flame of her candle a few times to complete the message, but the effort was worth it. The note said just what she wanted it to.

Satisfied and exhausted, Rapunzel ate a few bites of her soufflé and fell into a dreamless sleep.

Morning came quickly. Still curled up on her lumpy mattress, Rapunzel was suddenly aware of a blinding light. It burned right through her eyelids, giving her a headache. Was she dreaming?

Very slowly Rapunzel opened one eye. She wasn't dreaming. Her tower room was filled with a light so intense it hurt just to be in its presence. Using her hand to shade her eyes, Rapunzel looked around. She spied a bowl of boiled greens and a mug of tea on the table next to her bed.

"So much for better food," Rapunzel said, closing one eye and reaching for the fork. The greens were overdone and especially bitter.

By the time she had swallowed the last bite, Rapunzel could almost squint around her tower room without shading her eyes. Through lowered lids she saw a response from Madame Gothel written on the wall:

*Birds have wings. Bees have stings.*
*You, little bird, shall never fly.*

*You shall stay in this tower*
*Until the day you die.*

Rapunzel felt the blood pound through her veins.

"I will not be trapped! I will come and go as I please!" she shouted to no one. She hurried to the window to flee for the day. But if the light inside her tower was painfully bright, the light outside was truly blinding. It seemed as if all the sun's blazing energy were pinpointed on the stone tower in the forest.

Shielding her face with her arm, Rapunzel tried to look down to the ground. It was impossible. She couldn't see anything. Her head ached even more than before. Closing her eyes, she retreated into her tower room.

How was she going to get out of there?

Rapunzel tapped her foot on the stone floor in frustration. The soft sound echoed in her ears. And then she heard another sound — voices.

Familiar, friendly voices.

"Rapunzel!" Val shouted. "Are you okay? Stay away from the window! It's too bright!"

Relief flooded through Rapunzel. Then she smirked. "No kidding," she called back, teasing. "I thought it was midnight out there."

The next thing Rapunzel heard was a scraping sound — the sound of someone climbing up the tower.

But Val was terrified of heights. He'd only ever climbed up the tower once, and it had taken an hour of coaxing.

Then, all of a sudden, the light dimmed.

"Come on out," a different voice called. It was Rose. But the figure swinging its leg over the windowsill in Rapunzel's tower and successfully blocking the blinding light looked more like a knight. A knight wearing a dress.

Rose quickly pulled off Val's jousting helmet and tossed it to Rapunzel. She looked around at the tower room. "Put this on," she said matter-of-factly. "And pull the visor down to protect your eyes."

"What about you?" Rapunzel asked, taking the helmet. She was grateful for it, but wanted to make sure Rose had a plan for herself, too. "How will you see?"

Rose wrapped a gauzy scarf around her face several times. "I can use this," she said. "My eyes have adjusted a little. This will dim the brightness just enough."

Rapunzel pulled down the visor of the helmet and followed Rose out the window.

Climbing down wasn't easy. The bright sunlight made the tower stones scorching hot. Rapunzel kept banging the top of the visor on the tower wall. And Rose had to stop twice to retie the scarf around her eyes.

Finally Rose and Rapunzel stepped safely onto the ground.

Even under the shade of the forest trees it was still bright and unusually warm. But at least Rapunzel could see without the helmet. She pulled it off so she could recoil her hair. She handed the helmet to Rose. "Thanks," she said. "I could never have gotten down without —"

"A fine rescue, m'lady," Val said, interrupting Rapunzel. He took the helmet from Rose, then bowed low and kissed her hand. "Truly daring."

Rose giggled, and Rapunzel felt her thanks catch in her throat. She'd wanted to tell her friends everything about the letter mix-up and Madame Gothel's horrible reply. But not now. Clearly Rose hadn't come to help her. She was just trying to impress Val!

Without another word Rapunzel turned and stomped toward school.

# Chapter Nine
# Heating Up

Ella wiped her brow with the tiny lace handkerchief she kept in her sleeve and hurried down the road toward Princess School. She was late, and though the sun had only been up a few hours it was already blazing hot. Ella wished she had left her cloak at home, but after yesterday's hailstorm she hadn't known what to expect.

The weather was the least of Ella's worries. If she was tardy one more time she was not sure what Madame Garabaldi would do — probably pop her corset! But there was no way of getting out of her stepmother Kastrid's chores. That morning, in addition to the long list of usual tasks, Kastrid needed a dress pressed for a tea party she was hosting that afternoon, and her stepsisters Hagatha and Prunilla requested poached eggs *and* waffles for breakfast. And there would be more chores later, too, Ella was sure.

*What in the kingdom makes me think I can make it to*

*Rapunzel's tower next Monday to help Val?* Ella wondered.

Ella almost laughed at the idea of having "extra" time. But the thought of Rapunzel being stuck in her tower, unable to get to school, wiped the smile off her face. It was just too terrible to consider. Princess School needed Rapunzel. Ella needed Rapunzel. She was so fun and outspoken and spunky and bold — all of the things Ella wished she could be.

In the distance Ella heard the first trumpets peal. She only had a few minutes to get to hearthroom.

"Blast," she murmured, hoisting her skirts and hurrying faster.

Ella had reached the turnoff for the lane into town when a noise made her stop and turn. It sounded like branches scraping on windows. Or worse — Hagatha's laugh!

"Hagatha, don't you try to get me in trouble!" Ella called. There was no response. Maybe it was her other awful stepsister.

"Prunilla, you'll only make yourself late, too." Ella backed down the lane, looking right and left for Kastrid's nasty daughters. Despite the heat of the day, a chill went up Ella's spine. The screechy cackling sound was now directly to her left.

Whirling, Ella clapped her hand over her own

mouth to stifle a shriek. What she saw was worse than her stepsisters. Two nasty-looking Grimm witches were crouched in a stand of trees, waving twisted wands and laughing cruelly. In front of them a small whirlwind spun madly, throwing up sticks and dust and small rocks.

It was an impressive little tornado. But that wasn't what was making the witches cackle. A tiny, very scared-looking field mouse was caught in the vortex, squeaking for all he was worth as he was whirled around and around.

"Miserable mousie!" one of the witches mock-whined between guffaws. She had pond-water-colored hair and an orange-and-green-spotted dress. Ella couldn't see her face because she was bent over, clutching her stomach.

"Rotten rodent," the other witch chortled. The second voice was awfully familiar. Leaning farther forward, Ella spied the witch's black-and-red-striped stockings and lethal-looking boots. It could only be Hortense Hegbottom — one of the grisliest girls at Grimm School! Then Ella saw something lying by one of Hortense's huge boots. It looked like —

*Snap!* Suddenly a twig broke beneath Ella's soft slipper. All at once the cackling stopped. The two witches looked at each other, then turned in her direction. Ella did not stay to see if they saw her. Gathering her skirts, she ran toward Princess School as fast as she could.

As she slid into her hearthroom seat, Ella could still feel her heart pounding in her chest. She tried to quiet her breathing before Madame Garabaldi could point out that "panting is for poodles, not princesses." She could not wait to tell her friends what she had seen. She motioned Rose, Rapunzel, and Snow toward her.

"I think I know who's been messing with the weather," she puffed. "And mucking up the mail, too."

"Who?" Rose whispered.

"The Grimm witches!" Ella breathed. "I think you *did* see one with a scroll yesterday, Rose. I saw a pair on my way to school making whirlwinds and tormenting a field mouse. And I think I saw a scroll under Hortense's boot!"

"Hortense Hegbottom?" Rapunzel asked. Her face was contorted as if she smelled something foul.

Ella nodded.

"A field mouse?" Snow gasped.

Ella nodded again.

"There's something else —" Rose started to say. She was interrupted.

At the front of the room Madame Garabaldi took her throne and impatiently tapped her ringed fingers on the ornate arm.

"I hope I don't have to ask for your attention," she said softly. "Monarchs do not beg." The room went completely silent. The Bloomers knew better than to make Madame Garabaldi ask twice.

Pleased with the silence, Madame Garabaldi began scroll call. She announced each name as if she were reading from a grand guest list. "Rapunzel Arugula!" Rapunzel stood to answer.

Ella looked at Rose, a question in her eyes. What was the other news? Was it bad? Good? Rose pointed at Rapunzel under her desk and shook her head discreetly back and forth. Ella sighed. It looked as though there was more bad news about Rapunzel.

When Ella's name was called she stood and curtsied to Madame Garabaldi. "Present," she replied. Then she sat as patiently as she could until scroll call was over and Madame Garabaldi began the day's proclamations.

"As you all know, exams are quickly approaching. If you wish to improve your performance, as I am sure you all do" — Madame Garabaldi looked smilingly at her students — "I suggest you take advantage of your time here in hearthroom to prepare. In fact I suggest that you take every opportunity both at school and at home to study. These exams require only one thing — that you spend the time to prepare for them properly."

It was all Ella could do to keep from dropping her

head on her desk. *What time?* She barely had time to get to school, let alone study before and after!

*Maybe I should be the one locked in a tower,* Ella thought. *At least then I'd have a moment to myself!*

When Madame Garabaldi stood and turned toward her desk the princesses in hearthroom opened their texts. In an instant, Snow, Rose, and Rapunzel were huddled around Ella's desk.

"The little witches aren't the only ones mucking around," Rose whispered to her friends. "Gothel was trying to cook Rapunzel this morning. Val and I barely got her out!"

Rose related the whole story to Snow and Ella. When she finished, Snow's eyes were as big as saucers, and Ella had changed her mind about wanting to live in a tower.

"That's not all," Rapunzel said glumly. "Now Madame Gothel is acting like she really *is* my mother."

Ella cringed. She didn't think she could stand it if Kastrid started pretending she was her mother. And Kastrid wasn't even a real witch.

Rapunzel explained the letter mishap, twisting and untwisting her hair all the while. "She is flaming mad. And when she sees I am out of my tower again she's going to be even more determined to keep me in — forever!"

Ella was trying to think of something comforting to say when a trumpet blasted in the doorway, announcing a visitor.

"A thousand pardons!" Sir Spondence burst into the room followed by a page carrying a basket of scrolls. Madame Garabaldi rose slowly from her desk to greet the unexpected guest.

"To what do we owe the honor of your visit, Sir Spondence?" she asked. She didn't sound particularly honored.

"Good lady, I beseech you. Grant me but a moment to direct the deliverance of these late letters and I will trouble you no longer." Sir Spondence bowed low and smiled sweetly at the hearthroom teacher.

Madame Garabaldi did not return the smile, but she didn't banish the visitor, either. "Do it and be done," she said, waving her hand.

"Ah, gracious lady. May the stars —"

"Quickly," Madame Garabaldi enunciated.

Sir Spondence was uncharacteristically quiet as he took the scrolls from the page's basket and passed them to the girls.

"There are but a precious few," Sir Spondence whispered to all of the princesses looking expectantly at the basket. "A preponderance were pounded to a pulp by the hateful hailstones!"

Snow hastily opened the orangish scroll Sir Spondence had held out to her. "It's from Hans Charming!" she cried out.

"Of course it is, silly," Ella said in a hushed tone. Madame Garabaldi did not look up, but Ella could swear she saw her raise her eyebrows. "Didn't you write to him?"

"Yes, but he wants to meet me by the wishing well!" Snow burbled. "Ooh, Rapunzel, who wrote to you?"

Rapunzel had an unopened scroll on her desk, and Ella thought she looked a little nervous as she turned it over to examine the seal. It was a tiny dragon. "It's from Val," she said. She sounded surprised. And glad.

"But isn't your correspondent Oliver Eggert?" Ella asked.

"You know Val," Rapunzel said, ripping the scroll open. "He probably . . ." She trailed off.

Ella read the beginning of the letter over Rapunzel's shoulder. *My blooming Rose,* it began.

"That's not your letter," Ella said. Rapunzel must have realized the mix-up at the same moment because she quickly rerolled the scroll and thrust it toward Rose. But not before Ella read the next line. *I must speak to you* alone.

*What a prince!* Ella thought. Of course Val would be worried about Rapunzel. Of course he would want to ask Rose how to help.

Ella smiled, remembering how this same group of friends had gotten her through a tough time. They would do the same for Rapunzel. Together they could do anything!

Rapunzel did not seem so sure. She sat in front of Ella, staring straight ahead. Even though Ella couldn't see her face she could tell her friend was frowning.

"I'll come by on Monday to make sure you can get out," Ella whispered. She placed a reassuring hand on Rapunzel's shoulder. "Don't worry."

With all of her homework, extra studying, and chores to do, Ella didn't exactly know how she was going to make it to Rapunzel's on Monday morning. But she would. Rapunzel needed her, and Ella would not let her friend down.

## Chapter Ten
# Unraveling

When the final trumpet sounded, Rapunzel stood up slowly and filed with the other Bloomers into the unusually warm hallway. She had been listening all afternoon for the signal that the school day was over but now, facing a corridor of Bloomers bent over their trunks, she was not sure what she'd been waiting for. She certainly wasn't anxious to go home, especially since the sun was still blaring. What if she couldn't get into her tower? And assuming she could, the weekend loomed ahead of her like a waiting dragon.

Rapunzel pulled her embroidery hoop from her trunk. Her Stitchery project was going to make a terrible purse, but at least it was useful as a fan. She glanced up and down the corridor, scanning the faces for one of her friends. She needed cheering up.

She spotted Rose, surrounded by admiring girls, two trunks down. Rapunzel started to raise her hand.

Then she remembered the note in Val's scroll and pulled her hand back down like she'd touched fire. How could she forget Val was walking Rose home today — alone?

Ducking down so Rose wouldn't see her, Rapunzel fumed. It just wasn't fair. Val had been walking to and from school with her since the day she started Princess School. Princes were supposed to be loyal! And he wasn't just any prince, he was her friend — her oldest friend. If she couldn't count on Val, whom could she count on?

*Maybe Madame Gothel's right,* Rapunzel thought grimly. She felt her life was unraveling like an untied braid. *You have other friends*, she reminded herself. Hadn't Ella volunteered to come and make sure she got out on Monday morning? Rapunzel blew her bangs off her moist forehead. Monday was a long way off. And Rapunzel wanted to talk to somebody now.

The halls cleared out quickly as princesses collected their schoolwork and made their way toward waiting coaches. Rapunzel walked slowly several paces behind Rose. She'd walked right past Rapunzel without even noticing.

When they got outside, Rapunzel stopped on the stairs and watched Val introduce himself to Rose's father and her guardian fairies. *He probably has to talk them into letting Rose walk home!* Rapunzel thought.

Her father is probably terrified that she'll trip and stub her toe. She almost laughed. Living under such watchful eyes would drive Rapunzel crazy. But was it really that different from being locked in a tower?

Though Rose's father looked worried, eventually Rose and Val were allowed to walk together down the path toward Rose's castle. Rapunzel did notice one of the fairies — a blue one — flying a short distance behind. She tried again to laugh. Rose's parents treated her like such a baby! But she couldn't even smile. Her stomach was tied in knots, and watching Rose and Val together was only making the knots tighter.

Ella dashed past Rapunzel with a swish of worn taffeta, her arms full of books. "I'd love to walk home with you, but I have to get the tea and crumpets ready for Kastrid's party," she apologized. "And then I have to study!" She waved over her shoulder as she ran. Rapunzel was tempted to run beside her and tell her how awful she was feeling. She jogged a few steps but then stopped herself. Ella was such a good listener. But the poor girl had her own problems.

Besides, there was another person Rapunzel could talk to. If she hadn't rushed off, too.

"Is he there? Can you see him?" Snow's singsong voice was music to Rapunzel's ears. Snow was just coming out of the castle and gazing across the moat toward the Charm School.

"Who? Val?" Rapunzel asked.

"Oh, no!" Snow twittered. "Hans! Hans Charming. Do you see him by the wishing well? Do I look presentable?" Snow did a little curtsy demonstration for Rapunzel. She looked great but Rapunzel felt her heart sink. It was on a collision course with the knots in her stomach.

"Perfect," Rapunzel said a little glumly. She wasn't about to ruin Snow's first meeting with her pen-prince. So she kept her mouth shut and waved Snow off. "You'd better get to the well. Your prince will be there soon."

Snow skipped away, giggling. Rapunzel stood on the hot castle steps watching her last friend go. There was nothing left to do but head home.

Rapunzel's feet felt leaden on the woodland path. The sun beat down, making her coiled hair feel heavy on her head. Though she'd taken off her cloak she was sweltering under her gown.

*I don't think I have ever been this hot,* she mused. *Or this lonely*. The last thought echoed in Rapunzel's brain.

Before she started Princess School, Rapunzel didn't even know what lonely was. She had been alone for so much of her life it just felt normal. She used to entertain herself in her tower with whatever the wind happened to blow in her window — leaves, feathers, dandelion seeds. . . . Back then, spiders were her best companions. Then, when she was seven, Val had appeared and coaxed her down to the ground. And this year she'd started attending Princess School. Now, after having a taste of friendship, everything had changed. And not necessarily for the better.

When she reached the clearing, Rapunzel squinted up at her tower. The sun was lower and not nearly as bright as it had been that morning. But when Rapunzel touched the rounded rocks on the tower wall they were still hot. With no place else to go, Rapunzel climbed up quickly so she would not scorch her hands.

After pulling herself in the window Rapunzel collapsed on her bed. She closed her eyes but they could not shut out the thoughts whirling in her mind. She wished she could just stop thinking for a little while. When she opened her eyes again she saw her dinner sitting on the table — two toadstools and a handful of unwashed greens. Beside the dirty roots was another scroll from Madame Gothel.

*Rapunzel,*

*Toad's tears! Somehow you manage to get out of your tower in spite of me. Your ties of friendship must be very strong. Are they binding? You are right. I do not know much about friendship, but neither do you. I see all with my witch's sight. If you continue to escape you will receive a terrible slight.*

*M. Gothel*

Rapunzel cast the scroll across the room before she even read the last word. *What does that old hag know about my friends?* she fumed. Then she picked up the letter and read it again. *Toad's tears,* indeed!

Rapunzel grabbed the blackened stick from the hearth and wielded it over the back of the scroll like a weapon. She was about to start her reply when she heard a voice in her head. Not her own angry voice. A different one, a flowery one — Sir Spondence!

*'Tis true delight what courtly courtesy doth rend,* the instructor said.

Slowly a smile spread across Rapunzel's face. Her grasp around the stylus loosened, and she began to write.

*To the ever-thoughtful Madame Gothel,*

*However can I thank you for your kind letter of warning? Allow me to assure you that the salty offerings of a sad amphibian have nothing to do with my escaping the tower. As for my friends, I think I do know them. I am confident they will stand by me no matter what, for they are royally loyal.*

*Yours truly,*
*Rapunzel*

Satisfied, Rapunzel smoothed the scroll on the table and read it over one last time. It was certainly courteous. Sir Spondence would be proud. But with a pang Rapunzel wondered if her words were true.

*Of course my friends are royally loyal,* she reassured herself. *Aren't they?*

In a flash Rapunzel saw each of her friends rushing away from the Princess School steps, and away from her. Only a few days before, Rapunzel had been certain of her friendships. She couldn't have imagined doubting them. But everything was so topsy-turvy right now that Rapunzel didn't feel sure of anything.

# Chapter Eleven
# Secret Valentine

"Wow, they really look out for you, huh?" Val raised his eyebrows and nodded toward the blue fairy darting around Rose's head.

Rose batted at the fairy like a fly. "That's putting it mildly," she said. "Actually, I'm surprised they let me walk in the woods without more bodyguards than just Petunia."

"M'lady, you are safe in the presence of a prince." Val pulled a handkerchief from his waistcoat pocket and twirled it twice before bowing. When he stood up he was grinning.

Petunia crossed her teeny pudgy arms and *humphed* softly. She was obviously not sure about this "prince."

But Rose was. She admired the way his green eyes twinkled and gratefully took the handkerchief he offered. Daintily she dabbed tiny beads of perspiration from her brow. She could not wait to hear what Val wanted to talk to her about. But he'd said they needed to talk alone. And they weren't alone just yet.

Rose noticed Petunia was sweating and flying slowly. The heat must be getting to her, too. And it gave Rose an idea. Gently Rose held the handkerchief in the air for the fairy, and Petunia gratefully flew toward it to wipe her face.

"Oh, thank you, dear," the fairy squeaked, burying her whole head in the hanky. As soon as Petunia's eyes were covered Rose looked at Val and put a finger to her lips. Then she made two of her fingers walk quickly and pointed toward a bush. Rose loved Petunia. She was actually one of her favorites of the fairy pack. But right now she wanted to ditch her.

Val nodded his understanding and Rose quickly draped the handkerchief over Petunia's whole body, covering her — antennae to toes.

"Ack! Rose dear, what's happened? Where are you?" The fairy's tiny voice was muffled under the starched linen and the weight of it was pushing her down toward the forest floor. Rose stifled a giggle as she dove for the bushes. Val was right behind her.

"Oh, dear, oh, dear, oh, dear!" Petunia cried when she'd freed herself from the hanky. "Rose has been kid-napped! I must warn the king!" Petunia disappeared as fast as her small wings could propel her round body.

As soon as she was gone, the bush beside the trail erupted in laughter.

"I didn't know you had that in you!" Val said. He sounded impressed.

"I didn't, either." Rose laughed. "Poor Petunia!" Holding their stomachs, Val and Rose stumbled back onto the path.

"So, we're alone now. What did you want to talk to me about?" Rose asked. "And talk fast — it won't take Petunia long to tell my father I've been abducted!"

Rose dusted off her skirt and looked at Val sideways. She felt a little funny. Usually she hated to be around boys. They always acted so dippy. But Val was different. Besides the eyes, he was —

"I'm worried about Rapunzel," Val said. The laughter from a few seconds before was totally gone from his voice. His worry was genuine. "You know, she just hasn't been herself lately. And with Madame Gothel on her case, well . . . it's just that she used to be so carefree. I never worried about her. If anyone can handle living with a witch, it's Rapunzel. I mean, she always beats *me* in a fight." Val blushed a little and looked away from Rose. "But that was before. She doesn't seem so sure of herself now."

Rose nodded. She knew just what Val meant, but she was impressed that he'd noticed and that he cared so much.

"When we first met she had been alone for so long she couldn't even remember seeing anyone except for Madame Gothel, and maybe a Grimm girl going to school, or a woodsman passing by. She thought she made me up — like I was a figment of her imagination. She used to make up lots of games to make the time go by."

Val jumped up onto a large rock on the side of the path and pulled down an oak leaf. "She showed me how to make a kite with a leaf and a strand of hair." Val pulled a dark curled hair from his head to demonstrate. But it was too short and curly to tie to the leaf. "Her hair, of course. And she made up riddles, too. She can make fun out of thin air."

Rose just nodded as Val went on and on. She'd never thought about how alone Rapunzel was before she had Val.

"Most kids have toys and playmates and gardens and stables — lots of things to do. Rapunzel just had herself. She never even had a birthday party! She doesn't even know when her birthday *is*! I don't think she was ever very sad about it. You can't miss what you don't have. But the more time we spent together, the happier she got."

Val looked at Rose a little shyly. "And even then she wasn't as happy as she was when she made friends at Princess School." Val paused for a brief moment. "I guess what I'm saying is, we need to keep her spirits up or she won't have a chance against that old witch. I want to do something. I just don't know what."

Val, who had been walking and talking with increasing speed since he started his speech, came to an abrupt halt and let his hands drop to his sides. Rose bumped right into him. Her feet stopped but her mind was racing ahead. She couldn't believe everything she was hearing!

*No birthday party?* she thought. *Ever?*

Rose suddenly felt awful. She had always thought that Rapunzel had it easy in so many ways. She practically got to live by herself. She made her own rules. And nobody was ever looking over her shoulder.

But just that morning when Rose saw the tower room for the first time she had been shocked by how small it was. And now hearing Val, Rose had a new view. As much as Rose hated being coddled by her overprotective parents and pestering fairies, she couldn't imagine what it would be like if nobody *ever* made a fuss over her. Maybe that was just what Rapunzel needed. A little fuss.

"I've got it!" Rose grabbed Val by both his shoulders and looked into his surprised green eyes. "A birthday party!" she said. "We can throw Rapunzel a surprise birthday party."

Val's mouth dropped open, but he didn't say a word. He didn't have to. Rose was on a roll.

"It's perfect!" She clapped her hands together and started walking faster than ever down the path. "Snow and Ella will love it! Ooh, and I just remembered — soon we have to compose invitations for Cordial Correspondence. We can invite the other princes — Allister, Hans, and Oliver! And you, of course." Rose smiled over her shoulder at Val.

"It's a great idea!" Val grinned. "But we have to do it soon."

"We'll do it Monday," Rose said. "I can talk to the girls over the weekend."

"And I can teach you some of the flash signals so we can stay in touch about plans during school," Val said, catching Rose's enthusiasm. "It's going to work like a charm!"

The plan was perfect . . . except for one thing.

"It'll be great," Rose said thoughtfully. "Just as long as we can get our invitations properly delivered."

## Chapter Twelve

# Rising Waters

Rapunzel woke up staring at a bowl of acorns and torn lettuce. She rubbed her eyes. All night she'd dreamed of salad. Now her nightmare was sitting in a bowl beside her bed.

"About time you got up," Madame Gothel croaked. She was standing right next to Rapunzel's small table. Her arms were crossed and the green smoke that always marked her appearance was settling around her feet. She must have just arrived.

Hazy morning sunlight shone through the window, casting a ray onto the parchment on the table.

"Is this for me?" Madame Gothel asked. She picked up the polite response Rapunzel had written the night before, and with her back to Rapunzel began to read.

Rapunzel opened her mouth to speak, then closed it again. She had nothing to say to the old witch. At least not anything nice. Besides, she was curious to see what her reaction would be.

At first it was difficult to tell what Madame Gothel was thinking. Especially with her back turned. Then Madame Gothel's sharp shoulders started to creep closer to her ears. Her neck poked forward and Rapunzel could feel the sneer on her face. The witch was not amused.

The room grew darker as a rain cloud covered the morning sun. Madame Gothel whirled to face Rapunzel. Outside, rain began to fall.

"Troll snot!" she cursed. "What do you know about loyalty? You certainly don't know how to show it!"

Rapunzel's stomach clenched. "What do *you* know about my friends?" she replied, keeping her voice steady.

"I may not know them personally, but I know you won't be seeing them again," Madame Gothel growled back. "Not if I can help it."

Rapunzel looked at the floor. She wanted to hold her tongue and let Madame Gothel stew in her own juices. But she couldn't keep silent. "What do *you* know about *anything*?" she mumbled.

"Well, I *used* to know you, little girl." One of Madame Gothel's eyes grew narrower when she was mad. It was practically closed now. "There was a time when you were glad to see me. We had fun, you and I. Don't you remember anything I taught you?"

Madame Gothel reached out with gnarled fingers toward Rapunzel's braid. She strung a long lock through the fingers of both hands, leaving a little opening for Rapunzel to insert her own hand. It was an invitation to play Cat's Cradle, one of their favorite games when Rapunzel was younger. But Rapunzel had no interest in playing now.

She pulled her hair away and began to deftly fashion it into an elaborate tiara twist. Rapunzel did not look at Madame Gothel, but she could hear her cursing and fuming.

"Gnats! To think I taught you some of my best potions! Now you are so full of princess ways with your fancy hair and flowery speech. I . . . I barely know you!" Madame Gothel spat.

"Maybe you never did," Rapunzel spat back.

Madame Gothel's eyes burned. She did not wait for Rapunzel to unravel her hairdo and lower her out into the rain. Instead she waved her arms and disappeared in an angry cloud.

"And stay out," Rapunzel muttered, flopping down on her hard straw mattress.

Unfortunately, making Madame Gothel feel worse did not make Rapunzel feel any better. She knew it was foolish to make the witch angrier. It would only make her more determined to keep Rapunzel locked in her tower.

All through the long afternoon and evening, Rapunzel tried to study for her exams.

*After all of this work to stay in Princess School, I* can't *flunk out,* she thought with a wry smile. But she couldn't concentrate. She had no room in her head for memorizing the names of ancient monarchs. Every bit of her brain was consumed with worry — worry that she might never again see her friends or Princess School.

Time and again Rapunzel went to the window and peered out into the rain. It was never ending. And when she looked down at the base of her tower she saw the puddles starting to flow together. Water was inching its way up the rocks.

When Madame Gothel returned with Rapunzel's dinner of sour sorrel soup, the greens and acorns she'd brought for breakfast sat limp and uneaten right where the witch had left them.

Hiding her books under the mattress, Rapunzel pretended to be asleep. She heard Madame Gothel sit down on her small stool and let out a raspy sigh.

Rapunzel must have fallen asleep for real, because the next thing she knew it was morning. Though she could hear the rain falling on the thatched roof she hurried to the window and looked out, hoping for a change. Rapunzel felt her shoulders droop and her head tip forward. Things had changed all right.

Below her the water swirled faster and higher up the sides of the tower. The forest around her home was officially flooded. The flowers had been washed away. Bushes were almost entirely submerged. And small trees were in danger of drowning.

*I'll never get to school now,* Rapunzel thought, looking at the roiling waters. Even if her friends were as loyal as she hoped they were, how could they possibly get near her in this?

Rapunzel stared at the falling rain for the rest of the weekend. She gave up trying to study. She gave up eating. And she gave up hiding from Madame Gothel. When the witch appeared to bring breakfast and dinner that day Rapunzel did not pretend to be asleep. She didn't do anything but stare glumly out at the falling rain.

On Monday morning Madame Gothel arrived in a gray-and-red witch's dingy and moored it to the side of the tower with one of Rapunzel's braids. "Give up?" she asked, cackling as she tossed more wilted salad along with a few nuts and berries into Rapunzel's bowl.

"Never," Rapunzel said. But she said it more strongly than she felt it. Truthfully, Rapunzel nearly *had* given up. Though she had planned to swim for school that morning, whether her friends came through or not, a second glance at the churning floodwaters had changed her mind.

When Madame Gothel had gone, Rapunzel laid her chin in her hand. *There's no way Snow, Ella, Rose, or Val can make it through this mess,* she thought. She hoped the thought would comfort her. But it didn't convince her that her friends would come if they possibly could. She still felt alone and abandoned.

Wind sent the rain over the edge of the sill. It soaked into Rapunzel's skirts and dripped down her face like tears. Rapunzel squinted into the wicked weather and gasped. Straight ahead she saw a warm glow.

Rapunzel's jaw dropped when a purplish boat came into view. It looked a bit like an eggplant, and in the hands of the funny-looking, shimmery woman steering it, was a large wheel . . . of cheese.

"Hang on, dearie," the woman called. She was jerking the wheel this way and that in an attempt to steer the boat around trees and floating logs. Rapunzel wasn't sure who she was talking to, but the woman could certainly use the advice herself. The eggplant boat was turning in all different directions and looked in danger of capsizing as it zigzagged toward the tower through the frigid water.

"Rapunzel!" a familiar voice called. Behind the

woman steering the cheese, Rapunzel could just make out Ella's and Val's smiling faces. Ella was waving madly.

Suddenly the boat hit a snag. "Lurlina, look out!" Ella pitched forward. The boat almost careened into the tower, but Val reached forward and pushed the boat away from the stone wall. When she got to her feet, Ella was still smiling. "Ahoy!" she called.

Rapunzel returned her friend's grin before grabbing her texts and cloak, descending a foot or two, and leaping aboard. It wasn't a traditional rescue, but it would do.

## Chapter Thirteen
# Woodland Worry

Skipping outside, Snow stretched her arms and looked at the sky. The air felt electrified and the clouds above the treetops were an ominous gray-green.

"Thank goodness it stopped raining!" Snow chirped. Nearby, two bluebirds busily pulled worms from the drenched grass outside the dwarves' cottage. "Hello!" Snow called merrily. The birds looked up briefly, then turned back to their work. It had rained all weekend long, and they weren't sure what would happen with the weather next. They didn't have time to sing with Snow this morning. They needed to get food and get home!

"Bye-bye now," Snow called as the birds flew off. The busy birds and the gloomy clouds weren't enough to bring Snow down. She'd had a wonderful weekend, starting with her visit with Hans Charming at the wishing well. He was even more adorable than the dwarves! Then on Saturday morning, Rose and a pair of fairies had slogged their way to the cottage with some very exciting news.

Just thinking about Rose's news made Snow beam. She was planning a surprise party for Rapunzel! And Snow simply *loved* surprises.

"Oh, please, can I make the food?" Snow had pleaded.

Rose had easily agreed. And as soon as she did, Snow jumped up to begin. The rest of Snow's weekend was spent peeling and stirring, boiling and baking. The dwarves wanted to help, but Snow refused. She wanted to do everything herself as a special gift for Rapunzel. Snow had so much fun cooking that she almost forgot to study! Luckily Dim and Gruff were willing to help her there. They took turns holding her texts for her so she could read while she was rolling out dough or beating eggs.

Between the rain and the cooking, Snow hadn't made it outside in two days! "I wonder how my woodland friends are doing?" she said aloud. As soon as she'd spoken the words her smile faded. She had forgotten all about the forest animals. The grim weather had been particularly hard on them lately and she'd meant to check on a few of her favorite creatures to make sure they were okay.

Hoisting her skirts a little higher, Snow padded

over the sodden ground. She picked up her pace. If she hurried she would have time to look in on a few of her furry and feathered friends on her way to school.

"Robin!" Snow cooed, stopping by a low nest. "How is your wing?" The little bird's wing was newly healed. She looked well, if a little nervous. Snow stroked her feathers and skipped on.

"Hello, Buck," she spoke softly to a thicket. "Are you in there?" The young deer stepped shyly out of the bushes. He looked timid and shivery, but unhurt.

"Are you cold?" Snow asked. She touched his soft fur. It was wet through.

"Ooh, somebody ought to stop those bad Grimm girls from messing with the weather!" Snow said after stopping at the rabbit burrow and finding the bunnies huddled together to keep warm.

Snow stomped her slippered foot. It came down in the mud with an embarrassing squelch. For a moment Snow wished *she* had a way to stop the Grimm girls. Then she giggled at herself. The thought was preposterous. She couldn't even pass the gate to the Grimm School, let alone stand up to all of those witches! And with everything that was going on — the party planning, invitations, and exams — she wouldn't have the time even if she did have the nerve.

Slipping and scurrying, Snow hurried the rest of the way to school. She wondered about poor Rapunzel, shut up with that awful witch all weekend, and hoped she was okay — and that she got out this morning! Lately it seemed there was so much to worry about. But Snow could never fret for very long. There was always something to look forward to — and today it was a party!

As the spires of Princess School came into view, Snow spied Ella and Rose talking to another girl on the school steps. Though the other girl's back was to Snow, the telltale coil of hair made Snow clap her hands together with glee. Rapunzel had made it to school.

"Goody! You made it!" Snow cried as she rushed up to her friends.

"You should have seen it." Rapunzel's eyes were bright with exhilaration. "The water was practically up to my window, and suddenly a giant, floating, purple vegetable appears out of nowhere to rescue me!"

"Lurlina has a way with plants," Ella said humbly. "You should see what she can do with a tomato."

"Ella's fairy godmother is back," Rose explained to Snow, catching her up on the conversation.

"And just in time," Ella added. "She made a boat and helped get Rapunzel out this morning."

"Thank goodness," Snow said, giving herself a little hug. "If you hadn't made it to school we'd have had to cancel the pa —"

Rose stepped in front of Snow, cutting her off. "Say,

Ella, how did you get a fairy godmother, anyway?" she asked loudly. She gave Snow a look over her shoulder.

"Oops, I . . . I have to change my shoes!" Snow clamped her hand over her mouth and rushed up the stairs. She had almost blown the surprise in the first moment she'd seen Rapunzel! It was just too exciting.

*I've never been good at secrets*, Snow thought. She was just going to have to keep her distance in order to keep the party a surprise.

But staying away from Rapunzel was harder than Snow thought it would be. In hearthroom, Snow bent over her studies and tried not to look at any of her friends. She managed to keep her mouth closed, but she could not keep the smile off her face.

"*Psst*. Snow." Rapunzel leaned close to her ebony-haired friend. "Is the duke fourth or fifth in line for the crown in a kingdom without an heir?" she whispered.

Snow gulped. She looked at Rapunzel. The questioning look in Rapunzel's eyes was too much to take. Snow clamped her teeth together to hold back the secret waiting to burst out of her mouth.

"Frog got your tongue?" Rapunzel asked, looking at Snow a little sideways.

Snow looked back at her desk. Luckily, the trumpet sounded at that very moment. Snow jumped to her feet and ran for her trunk. It was a close call.

Correspondence class was even harder. Not only did Snow have to keep the party a secret, she had to make her invitation for Hans Charming without Rapunzel seeing it! She leaned close to her desk, using her dark hair as a curtain. She wrote quickly, not in her best script, and with a quick glance to see if anyone noticed, she sealed the scroll and breathed a small sigh of relief.

Sir Spondence was strangely silent. Usually he strolled around the chamber exclaiming over a fine seal or a sweet turn of phrase. Today he just stood at the front, gazing out the window and tugging his goatee.

When the missives were ready for delivery, Sir Spondence led the girls down the spiral staircases to the grand foyer. Snow hung back. She did not want to walk beside Rapunzel.

The school doors whooshed open. Outside, the clouds felt lower and darker than they had that morning. But the thick air could not hold Snow's excitement down. She hopped over puddles like a bunny, and when Rapunzel paused to ask Sir Spondence a question, Snow sprang ahead to catch up with Ella and Rose.

"Do you think she knows?" Snow whispered.

Ella and Rose looked toward Rapunzel. They didn't

know what she had asked the instructor, but she was scowling at the answer.

"Not yet," Rose said. "But let's stick together until these invitations get out. We don't want to ruin the surprise."

At the willow, a flock of mourning doves was perched and cooing softly.

"Ooh, doves!" Snow giggled. She'd been looking forward to trying winged delivery.

With their shoulders pressed tightly together, Snow, Ella, and Rose tied their scrolls around the birds' legs.

"I wrote my invitation to Oliver," Rose explained. "Val already knows all about the party."

Ella nodded. Snow let another giggle escape. She glanced over her shoulder and saw Rapunzel's scowl deepen. "Rapunzel needs a party. I hope this works," Snow whispered.

Rose still looked serious. "Me, too," she said quietly, holding her dove up on one finger. "The princes have to get the invitations today!"

Rapunzel sidled closer and the other girls stopped talking. "Is it almost lunchtime?" Rapunzel asked grumpily. "I am starved. And it had better not be salad. What I wouldn't give for a slice of pie."

Ella, Rose, and Snow exchanged glances.

Snow lifted her dove into the air and watched it fly toward the dark clouds. She bit her bottom lip. It was all she could do to keep from telling Rapunzel about the delicious apple and berry pies waiting for her — and her party!

## Chapter Fourteen
# News Flash!

Rapunzel was in a mood. Her face looked as dark as the storm clouds hanging over Princess School. She had grumbled all through lunch in the banquet hall and now, in Looking Glass class, the look she was giving her reflection was almost enough to break the mirror.

Rose knew her friend was dealing with enough to make any princess cross. But Rapunzel's disposition was positively ferocious. Rose hoped the party would be *enough* to cheer her up — and that Rapunzel wouldn't do anything drastic before then!

Under the circumstances, Snow's tactic of steering clear of their friend until the surprise seemed like a good idea. Rose turned her cushioned stool so she couldn't see Rapunzel. Then she arranged a spiral curl down the nape of her neck.

A quick flash of light in her mirror made Rose close her eyes briefly. What was that? A second flash followed. Then two more in quick succession. It was a signal. Val!

Rose glanced around the chamber to see if Rapunzel had noticed. She and the other princesses were busy trying to perfect their curls. Snow's stick-straight hair was hopeless!

Sliding off her cushion, Rose made her way to the window ledge and the cut-glass jar filled with hair combs. Pretending to pick a new comb, Rose snuck a look out the window. It was Val all right. He was standing on the Charm School lawn tilting his shiny belt buckle this way and that in an effort to catch a ray of light. The sky was still cloudy, so he had to wait for small breaks in the building storm.

*He must be desperate if he is trying to signal me now!* Rose thought. She racked her brain trying to remember the parts of the code he'd tried to teach her on their brief walk.

*Was it two flashes for "meet in the stables"? Or two quick, one long?* Rose asked herself. She could not remember. And there was only one other person who would know.

Rapunzel had a single lock of her long hair wrapped around a heated iron. It circled the metal so many times it looked like a ball of yarn. She unwrapped it as Rose approached, and only an inch at the end had curled. The rest hung straight.

"Lovely," Rapunzel muttered sarcastically.

"I like your hair better braided anyway," Rose said, smiling widely.

Rapunzel rolled her eyes. "And how does Val like *your* hair?" she asked. Her voice was full of sarcasm.

This was going to be trickier than Rose thought. She had suspected Rapunzel was angry that Val had walked home with her the other day. But she'd hoped she would be over it by now. Besides, all they had talked about was her!

"Val doesn't talk about hair," Rose said lightly. "But he did tell me about the code you created. I think it's so clever that you two can talk while you're in two different schools! How did you come up with it?"

Rapunzel looked at Rose suspiciously. "I don't know. I just did, I guess."

"It's just *so* clever," Rose went on, using a tone she usually reserved for talking her parents into something. She knew flattery was a powerful tool, but she'd never tried it on Rapunzel. And her friend was looking royally annoyed! "Can't you tell me some of the things the code says?"

Rapunzel put her hairbrush down on the dressing table with a thud. "It's simple. Anybody could do it. One flash means 'yes.' Two means 'no.' It's very basic." Rapunzel sighed.

Light flashed again in the mirror behind Rapunzel —

two long, two short. Rose hoped Rapunzel hadn't seen it, too. She just had to figure out what Val was trying to tell her before Rapunzel caught on!

"So, what would two long and two short mean?" Rose blurted. She felt like her smile was plastered to her face.

Rapunzel narrowed her eyes. She suspected something. "It would mean 'trouble,'" she said. "Why?"

"Oh, no reason," Rose said, waving a hand in the air. She hoped Rapunzel couldn't see her face starting to flush.

"Who's in trouble?" Ella peeked around Rapunzel's looking glass. Her hair cascaded in yellow curls around her face.

"Nobody!" Rose said quickly. Ella's distraction came just in time! "Ella, your hair looks perfect. You just need a comb over your ear. I saw one with a butterfly over here."

Rose led Ella back toward the window. "Something's gone wrong," she whispered when they were far enough from Rapunzel. "Val is telling me there's trouble."

While Ella pretended to busy herself with the combs, Rose peered down at Val. When he saw her face in the window, he dropped his belt buckle completely and signaled frantically with his hands. He held up three fingers, then two. He held up three again and covered one with his hand. At last he pulled a scroll from his pocket and pointed to it, then gestured like a court magician making something disappear.

"It's the invitations," Rose whispered frantically. Her fears had been confirmed. "One of them is missing!"

## Chapter Fifteen

# A Change of Scenery

Rapunzel's mind raced like a stolen coach. Everything around her was so strange, starting with the weather and ending with her friends. Wasn't it enough that she had to contend with a witch at home? Why did everything have to spin out of control at once?

Making her way toward the Self-Defense classroom, Rapunzel felt grateful for her assigned princess duty. There would be no wolf evasion practice today. Today she would be there by herself. And all she had to do was switch the scenery. Maybe because she spent so much time alone growing up, Rapunzel felt she did her best thinking that way. And she had lots to think about.

"Rapunzel! Wait for me!" Arinda, the miller's daughter, ran down the hall. "I have scene-changing duty, too. I saw your name on the roster. Isn't it great to have a free period? I have been studying so much lately. Not that I'm worried about the exams. My father says I can do anything! So I'm sure to get a golden mark."

Rapunzel glanced at the girl chatting rapidly by her side. So much for a moment to think! Arinda was always talking. And most of the time she was bragging, too. *Someday her bragging is going to get her into trouble,* Rapunzel thought.

Pushing open the door to the large hall where the princesses learned to protect themselves, Rapunzel spotted the woodland props. Trees and bushes and rocks were placed around the room to imitate a forest path. They needed to be taken down and replaced with village scenery.

"Would you like to see my skip-trip?" Arinda asked, eyeing the forest. "It's practically a flip. My father says I could take down a whole pack of wolves with it and the woodsman, too."

Rapunzel wrestled the bush toward a large storage compartment. *If I don't reply she might stop talking,* Rapunzel thought. Her head was crowded enough without Arinda's crowing!

Rapunzel pushed the bush to the back of the compartment and pulled out a village stall, one of the props used to create a mock town lane.

"I heard we're taking on rats and pipers in Self-Defense next," Arinda kept on. "That should be no problem for me. I'm not afraid of rats. And Father says I'm very musical. Practically a lark, he says."

Arinda kept talking. But Rapunzel found if she held a prop between herself and the chatterbox, she could hear her own thoughts in spite of Arinda's constant din. But as soon as she heard the doubts about her friends and Madame Gothel flooding back, she wished they were drowned out again. Rapunzel was confused. And sad. And angry. She didn't want Madame Gothel to be right about her friends. But maybe she was. Maybe they would disappoint and leave her. Just like her parents.

*Ella and Lurlina* did *come to get me out*, she reminded herself. She was grateful for that. But Ella had seemed distant since then. And what was with Rose? It wasn't enough that Rose was walking home with Val and Rapunzel was walking alone. Now Rose wanted to know their secret code, too. The one Rapunzel had made up!

Then there was Snow. She always acted a little funny. Rapunzel thought it was because she lived with dwarves. But today? Every time she looked at Rapunzel she looked like she'd swallowed a toad. Rapunzel set a stile prop on her foot.

*Ouch!* She would have thought that Snow of all people would understand what it was like living with a witch.

But the thing that had felt the worst was when all three of her friends completely ignored her during Cordial Correspondence. They kept their backs to her and didn't ask her to tie scrolls with them. She might as well stay locked in a tower if this was how her friends were going to treat her!

All she'd wanted was to talk to them about the awful food and letters Madame Gothel had been leaving her. She'd tried again at lunch to tell them. She'd started by saying she hadn't gotten any studying done. "I'm going to have to spend at least two hours in the royal library after school today," she'd confided. Then she had actually seen the girls exchange smiles — like they were happy she wasn't going to do well! And nobody had said a thing. She felt like her friends didn't listen anymore — or worse, didn't care! It was enough to make Rapunzel stop talking.

Arinda, on the other hand, *never* stopped talking. "I think this is the best village setup ever. Except for that crooked stile over there. Did you put that up, Rapunzel? Don't worry, I can fix it. Father says I have an eye for arranging. I can spot a flaw no matter how slight."

As Rapunzel pushed the last tree into the storage compartment, Madame Gothel's words echoed in her head. *Continue to escape and you will receive a terrible slight.* Was her friends' aloofness the slight Madame

Gothel was talking about? She said her friends would betray and forget her. Was that what was happening?

"No," Rapunzel said aloud.

"Oh, yes." Arinda nodded vigorously. "And I can feel a grain of sand under twenty mattresses."

"I don't believe it," Rapunzel said to herself. She had to give her friends another chance. Dusting her hands on her skirt, Rapunzel headed for the door.

"It's true. Every word!" Arinda called after her.

But Rapunzel didn't hear her. All she needed was a moment alone with one of her friends. Just a few minutes to talk and she knew she would feel better.

The trumpet blasted as Rapunzel entered the corridor and the halls filled with swirling skirts and sweet voices. It didn't take long to spot Snow and Rose, but they were headed outside and Rapunzel was too far away to catch up to them through the crowd.

Rapunzel waited by Ella's trunk, watching as the last princesses filed outside. Still no Ella. A new and terrible thought stormed into Rapunzel's head. They all were avoiding her — on purpose!

Feeling wilted, Rapunzel pulled her scrolls and texts from her own trunk and let the lid slam with a bang. *Fine*, she thought. *I don't need those traitors. I don't need anybody!*

Rapunzel stomped toward the cupola that held

the royal library. She yanked the door open with a vengeance and was surprised to be greeted by a friendly face — Ella.

"There you are!" Ella grinned. "I was hoping to have someone to study with."

Rapunzel felt her anger start to thaw the moment she saw Ella. She desperately wanted to be wrong about her friends. She also desperately wanted to talk to someone about the maelstrom of feelings she had been having.

"I'm glad you're here," Rapunzel said as she followed Ella to a carved, round table. The huge multilevel chamber was quiet. Enormous pastel-colored banners hung down from second-level banisters. And shelves upon shelves of books spread out of the circle room like spokes.

"Me, too." Ella nodded. "I think this may be my only chance to study for exams. I have been so busy with chores I haven't even had a minute to myself! You're so lucky you live alone!"

Rapunzel snorted. Was she joking?

Ella sat down daintily in a high-back chair, opened her text, and began to read. The look on her face was pure concentration.

Sinking into her own chair, Rapunzel felt frustration fill her once more. With a sigh, she spread her own text on the table and began to read in silence.

# Chapter Sixteen
# Snow Storm

Snow nibbled on the corner of her thumbnail and glanced anxiously around for Val.

"He'll be here," Rose assured her, leaning on the rail of the Princess School drawbridge. Rose held up her arms like an arch and raised one slightly in imitation of Val's pantomime. "I'm almost certain he was saying 'bridge.'"

Snow nodded and tried to smile. All of her excitement about the party had turned to nervousness. It seemed as though everything was starting to go wrong. Ever since Rose told her that one of the invitations was missing, Snow had been trying not to panic.

*It could be anywhere*, Snow thought. *The doves could have given it to Rapunzel and ruined the surprise. Or worse.* Both of Snow's hands crept toward her ruby-red lips. *The invitation could be in the clutches of a Grimm girl!*

The clouds overhead that had been building since

the early morning seemed darker now. And in the distance, Snow thought she heard the rumble of thunder.

"Hey, are you trembling?" Rose put her hand on Snow's shoulder. "There's no need to panic, Snow. Val is on his way and Ella is with Rapunzel. We'll have plenty of time to get the food and get to the tower. Rapunzel doesn't suspect a thing."

Rose's reassuring words helped Snow relax a little. She took a deep breath and let her hands drop to her sides. She admired Rose's coolheadedness. And Rose was right, Snow knew. Ella was with Rapunzel in the library and under strict orders to keep her there for at least an hour. They had time.

"Sorry I'm late!" Val galloped up the path toward Rose and Snow, pausing to tip his crown and bow slightly when he drew near. "I just had to give the princes directions. They asked me to relate that they are most honored to be invited and will certainly be attending."

"Did you find the missing invitation?" Rose asked.

"No, Oliver never got one. But he's coming. You should have seen his face when I told him you would be there." Val grinned.

"Okay, let's go!" Rose said, rolling her eyes. She walked briskly toward the willow and the path to Snow's cottage, gracefully leaping and dodging puddles on the way. Val tried to walk ahead of her and when Rose paused at the edge of a big puddle, even offered to lay his cloak on top of it so that she and Snow could walk across it.

"No time for gallantry," Rose said, waving Val off with her hand. She gathered her skirts and leaped the puddle easily. Val jumped after her and came down on the edge, splashing his boots and making them both laugh.

Snow smiled, but she couldn't seem to catch her friends' playful mood. She accepted Val's hand and made it across the huge puddle herself. As she landed, something behind the trunk of the willow caught her eye.

Crouching, Snow peeked cautiously around the tree. Five small rabbits were huddled together, shivering and looking up at the sky as if it were about to fall on their fuzzy heads. They were frightened and muddy.

"Oh, you poor bunnies!" Snow scooped the rabbits into her skirts and dried them off with her hem. "Just look at them, Rose!"

Rose was already at the edge of the woods, but she came back and crouched beside Snow. She gently stroked one of the rabbits while Val leaned over her shoulder.

"What's wrong with them?" Val asked.

"They're frightened," Snow said, kissing the tops of their heads and making soft sounds in their long ears. "Has all this awful weather scared you?" She looked into the smallest rabbit's dewy eyes.

A mother deer and her fawn stepped timidly under the umbrella of the willow tree. They looked disheveled and upset as well.

"You, too?" Snow asked. Her voice was full of sympathy.

Suddenly the rabbits cowered further into Snow's skirts and the deer stood stock-still, clearly startled. There was a rustling overhead. "Ooh, that mean old thunder!" Snow frowned.

But the noise above them wasn't thunder. Three mourning doves flapped ungracefully down to roost in the willow.

"Aren't those the birds we sent to Charm School?" Rose asked. "Maybe they have the lost invitation!"

*Finally, some hope!* Snow thought. She tucked the rabbits into a dry knothole and held a hand up so the doves could fly closer. Two of them flew down to rest on Snow's outstretched arm. The third landed on her head. All of them wobbled woozily back and forth.

"Why, you're all worn out from the weather, too," Snow cooed.

"And if they did have that other invitation, they don't anymore," Rose pointed out. "I guess there's nothing left to do but go to the party and hope we don't have an uninvited guest."

Rose started toward the path with Val right behind

her, but Snow didn't move. She was trembling again. But this time she wasn't nervous. The gentle girl trembled with rage.

"It's those Grimm girls," Snow said in a tone her friends had never heard her use. "They're the ones. They are trying to mix up our mail with their bewitched weather, and they are frightening the animals. It's just not right."

Snow balled her delicate hands into tight fists. The animals that usually flocked to her looked shocked and kept their distance.

"Mischief is one thing," Snow said. She felt hot tears burning her eyes. "This is mistreatment, and I won't stand for it."

"They'll be okay, Snow," Rose said, trying to calm her. "Let's just get to the cottage and get the food for the party. You'll feel better then."

"No," Snow said more sternly than she'd meant to. Rose looked taken aback and Val stood with his mouth open. Snow knew she wasn't acting like her usual self — she was surprised, too. But she wasn't going to let her woodland friends be abused another moment.

"You go to the cottage," Snow said commandingly. "Pick up the food, then get to the tower and make sure everything's ready. I'm going to find Sir Spondence. Somebody has to put a stop to this. Now."

## Chapter Seventeen
# Ill Wind

*When taking tea, a proper princess always extends her pinkie so that when the cup is tipped her smallest digit points directly at the ceiling.*

*Huh*, Ella sighed. Though she would never tell an instructor, sometimes all of the princess protocol seemed to her like utter nonsense. Here she was trying to plan a party, stay out of trouble with her steps, and rescue her friend from the doldrums (and a witch). Was she really expected to memorize perfect pinkie positioning? It all seemed a little preposterous.

But even if what she was studying were more important, Ella knew she'd still have trouble concentrating. Rapunzel's miserable silence across the table was setting off alarms in Ella's head. She knew Rapunzel wanted to talk, wanted to ask a million questions. And she had every right to.

Ella hoped that Rapunzel would understand why she was being so coy when she saw what she and the others had been up to. They were trying to be good friends. But right now, from under Rapunzel's heavy hair, Ella knew it looked bad.

Gnawing on her quill, Rapunzel glared at her text. She stood quickly, knocking over her chair and getting a few looks of shock and displeasure from the ladies-in-waiting at the Table of Information.

"Where are you going?" Ella asked abruptly. They had only been in the library a short while and she was supposed to keep Rapunzel occupied for at least an hour!

"The little princesses' room," Rapunzel whispered loudly. Ella thought she saw her roll her eyes. She could follow her, but it might seem suspicious. And she didn't want Rapunzel to start asking questions now, with the party so close. She would just have to let her go.

Trying again to focus on her princess protocol text, Ella was surprised to see familiar slippers appear on the floor beside her.

"Come with me!" Snow whispered hoarsely. She grabbed Ella's arm and started to drag her out of the library.

"Snow! What is it? What's happened?" Ella ran behind Snow to avoid being pulled across the room. The pale girl was surprisingly strong!

"The animals!" Snow said as if Ella should already

know. "We have to talk to Sir Spondence about what the Grimms are doing to the animals."

"The animals?" Ella asked, unwrapping Snow's hand from her puffy sleeve.

"They are completely shaken from this unpredictable weather! You should see them, Ella. They're shivering and terrified." Snow stopped and looked into Ella's face. "We have to do something."

Ella had only seen sweet, cheery Snow this distraught once before, when she had been hiding under the bleachers at the Maiden Games. She'd been afraid to move, afraid to face the evil Malodora. She didn't seem fearful now.

"You saw them do it. You saw those girls make that terrible twister to mix up our mail. That's why you should be the one to tell Sir Spondence." Snow shoved Ella into the Cordial Correspondence classroom ahead of her. Sir Spondence was leaning back in his chair, asleep.

"What about the party?" Ella whispered.

"There will be time for that later." Snow picked up a stick of sealing wax and dropped it on the floor with a clatter.

"Heavens! Gracious!" Sir Spondence was startled awake and blinked at his two students. "Good afternoon! What have we here? I was just in a reverie. I dozed and dreamed that all of the epistles . . ." He shook his head mournfully. "Would that I knew what had happened to our wayward words."

Ella felt Snow nudge her firmly in the back. "I saw two Grimm girls casting weather spells in the woods!" Ella said abruptly.

Sir Spondence rubbed his eyes and tugged on his goatee harder than ever.

"Sir Spondence, sir," Snow pleaded. "One of our scrolls was there. The lost letters and horrible weather might be the Grimms' fault, and it's harming the innocent animals!" She stepped closer to the instructor, grasped the hem of his elbow-length cape, and looked at him with her round ebony eyes. "We have to do something."

The teacher shook his head as if waking a second time, got to his feet, and strode out of the room. "Quite right," he said crisply. "Right. Quite!"

Ella and Snow were close on his heels. "Where are you going?" Snow called, running after him. She still held the corner of his short cape.

"Perchance to see what foul players prey upon our fowl," Sir Spondence grumbled. "Could it be that the School of Grimm should conduct their course in Malicious Mischief at the same moment I conduct mine in Cordial Correspondence? Rest assured that if it *is* their ill wind that blows our letters astray I will put a stop to it!"

As they walked quickly away from Princess School, Ella heard a clock tower strike the hour. It was getting late. The party would be starting soon and Ella hoped Rapunzel wasn't going to be the one surprising Rose and Val!

Ella struggled to keep up with Snow and Sir Spondence. The closer they got to the Grimm School's grimy castle, the darker the woods got. The clouds looked caught in the tops of the gnarled trees and more and more roots twisted their way into the path to trip passersby.

Snow did not slow her pace as they made their way through the woods. But when Sir Spondence reached the frosted gingerbread gate that marked the boundary of the Grimm School yard, Snow stopped so suddenly Ella ran right into her.

"Oof." Ella stumbled back. "Snow, what is it?"

"Nothing," Snow said softly. Ella heard her draw in her breath. She knew what it was. Snow was scared. No amount of gingerbread or candy would make her set foot on Grimm School grounds. Her stepmother, the evil Malodora, was headmistress there. Snow had stood up to Malodora at the Maiden Games, but that was completely different from setting foot in her stepmother's territory.

Sir Spondence was halfway to the castle doors, and Ella wanted to catch up with him. She wasn't exactly feeling brave about hanging out in the witches' woods without her teacher. She opened her mouth to remind Snow they were there for her animal friends. But she didn't need to.

Snow let her breath out slowly, squared her shoulders, and stepped through the frosted gates.

A moment later they were at the entrance. The doors to the Grimm School were enormous — even bigger than the grand Princess School doors. The leering door knocker was almost too high for even Sir Spondence to reach. He stood on his tiptoes and grabbed the tarnished ring that hung from the mouth of a grimacing gargoyle. The gargoyle appeared to recoil slightly at being touched by a white-gloved hand.

Sir Spondence let the ring fall. The clang of metal on metal echoed inside. Ella wanted to run, but her feet wouldn't move. Even Sir Spondence was starting to look a little nervous.

At last the doors opened and Ella, Snow, and Sir Spondence were enveloped in a cloud of warm, stagnant air. Ella felt like the school had just belched in their faces. And the smell!

"What a stench!" Sir Spondence whispered. Princesses, cover your noses. Let not the reek of sorceresses enter your dainty nostrils." He produced several lace handkerchiefs and handed one to Ella and one to Snow. Ella gratefully covered her face before stepping inside the empty hall. Her handkerchief smelled like vanilla but could not cover the rank odor of sulfur and mildew mingling in the Grimm hallway.

Ella and Snow had to hurry to keep up with Sir Spondence. Face covered, he marched smartly down the hall, looking left and right into rooms filled with dusty texts and bottles of fetid potions. Snow slipped along on the slimy floor and Ella linked arms with her.

"Thank you," Snow murmured under her hanky. Ella nodded back but didn't say anything. She was hanging on to Snow as much for herself as for her friend. The empty hallways were giving her the creeps.

Suddenly something limped toward them. A bent witch with a crumpled hat and a twisted walking stick looked at them through one eye. The other was sealed shut. "What do you want?" she snarled.

"I seek an audience with someone in a position of power," Sir Spondence said formally. He started to bow, but seemed to think better of lowering his balding head before a witch holding a stick.

"Ha!" the old witch laughed, revealing yellowed and broken teeth. Her laugh caught in her throat, choking her. She started to hack, bending farther, but as she coughed she pointed with her stick toward a door leaning on its hinges. The splintery sign on it read JEZEBEL JEWELWEED.

Sir Spondence turned and gestured for Ella and Snow to stay close. Behind them the short witch's hacking echoed in the dank hall.

Using one of his handkerchiefs, Sir Spondence grasped the door handle and pushed his way inside the office. A silver-haired hag sat at an enormous desk. Though Sir Spondence cleared his throat, she did not look up when they entered. Instead she stared intently into a glowing crystal ball. Her long, silvery fingers moved near the shining surface, never touching the glass.

If Ella was frightened before, she was petrified now. She squeezed Snow's arm tighter. Snow wasn't even shivering.

Sir Spondence puffed out his chest and prepared to speak. "If you will excuse the intrusion, Madame Jewelweed, I —" He was cut off by a snort.

"Silence," the witch commanded, looking up from her ball. She surveyed the three royals before her with distaste. "Your saccharine speech will only give me a toothache. Besides, I know why you're here. And you're mostly wrong."

Ella looked at Snow, who did not look as surprised as Ella felt. But then Snow's stepmother was a powerful witch who used a mirror to know all. This witch must use a crystal ball the same way.

Jezebel Jewelweed stood and walked closer to Sir Spondence. She pulled his hand down from his face, uncovering his protected nose and mouth.

"Of course we would be proud if our little brats could cast such strong weather spells," she hissed. "As it is, they have simply been interfering a tiny bit with your foolish postal play — something we choose to allow. Every good witch stirs up trouble, after all."

Sir Spondence began to stammer. Jezebel put a gnarled knuckle on his lips. "Dear sir," she mocked him. "The spells you seek are beyond the capability of any Grimm student."

The hag chuckled and turned her attention from Sir Spondence to Snow and Ella, who stood almost hugging behind him. "The spells you speak of could only be created by an unusually powerful witch — a witch in danger of losing something she holds dear," she said softly. Ella felt Jezebel's gaze bore into her and shuddered. The witch's eerie smile grew. "A witch about to do something drastic," she added.

Ella wasn't sure if Snow pulled her or she pulled Snow, but the next thing she knew, both of them were bolting down the slimy halls, past the gingerbread gates, and down the path toward Rapunzel's tower.

# Chapter Eighteen
# Surprise!

By the time she reached the tower, Rose was completely out of breath. She stopped in the small clearing and put her hands on her knees. Panting wasn't very princessy, but neither was pushing a wooden cart of pies and cookies down a woodland trail!

Val bumped to a stop beside her. "Can I eat one now?" he asked, eyeing one of the cookies in the wheelbarrow.

"Not yet," Rose breathed. She pushed the cart behind a small bush in case Rapunzel showed up early. "We have to get them into the tower first." She gestured toward Rapunzel's open window thirty feet above them and let her eyes follow. The last time she was here the tower had been bathed in such bright light she could barely look at it. This time it was dark. Thick clouds swirled menacingly above the pointed roof, blocking all light save the greenish-gray glow of the sky before a storm.

Though she was still warm and flushed from hurrying down the trail, Rose shivered. The tower looked pretty spooky. But something else was bothering her, too. She couldn't shake the odd feeling in the pit of her stomach. And she couldn't name it, either.

"We have to get all this up there?" Val pointed straight up in the air. He didn't look like he felt very well. "Can't we just have the party down here?"

"Don't worry. I'll help you up." Rose walked closer to the tower and found her first toehold. "Then we can make some sort of pulley system for the rest."

Val started to shake his head but a crash in the bushes made them both jump. Rose looked for someplace to hide but it was too late. A pair of twig-covered figures stumbled out of the woods. Snow and Ella! Their cheeks were rosy and they were breathing as hard as Rose had been a minute before.

"Is she with you?" Ella gasped.

"Rapunzel?" Val asked.

"I thought she was with you!" Rose said. The odd feeling in her stomach felt like panic now.

Suddenly an auburn braid sailed out of the tower window and swung to a stop by Rose's side.

"Are you going to just stand down there all day?" Rapunzel's voice sounded like music to Rose's ears.

"I guess she got here before us," Val said, scratching his head. He looked a little disappointed.

"Climb on up!" The braid jiggled. "The others are already here. Let's get the party started!"

"So much for the surprise." Ella shrugged and started to climb.

"At least we're all together," Snow said, looking on the bright side. She stepped forward and hoisted herself onto the ropy braid.

When Snow was about ten feet up, Rose pushed Val to go next.

"I'll be right behind you." Rose tried to sound reassuring, but she wasn't feeling very sure herself. She knew she could climb up without a problem. But the uneasy feeling in her stomach was still there.

Rose helped Val position his feet, wrapping the braid around his waist so he'd be safe if he fell. "I still don't understand why we couldn't have this party on the ground!" he said in a shaky voice.

"Because it's not your party," Rose said. "Now keep climbing!" She tried to concentrate on the next handhold but a voice was clamoring in her head and getting louder all the time.

*How'd she get here before we did? If she knew about the party at school, why didn't she just tell us?* Rose didn't think it was like Rapunzel to be secretive.

Above them, Snow and Ella had reached the windowsill and climbed over. Rose thought she heard a gasp. Suddenly Val started to slip. His foot came down on Rose's head.

"Use the braid," Rose said through clenched teeth. For a charming prince, Val was a terrible climber. Taking Val's suede boot in her hand, Rose pushed up hard and foisted him in through the open window. She swung easily in beside him and gasped herself.

A stern-looking woman with a sharp nose and a witch's cloak stood beside the window glowering at the royal students assembled in the tiny tower room. She leaned on the end of a hard bed where the auburn rope Rose had just climbed was knotted. Behind her, three frightened princes sat bound together. It was a trap. The woman could only be Madame Gothel!

The witch's glower snaked itself into a sinister smile. "Well, if it isn't my *friends*!" she said in a perfect imitation of Rapunzel's voice. Throwing her head back, she cackled madly. And at the same moment a booming thunderclap echoed in the darkened sky.

## Chapter Nineteen
# Party

Rapunzel kicked the dirt, scuffling her way home. She had been hoping that when she went to the little princesses' room Ella would follow her so they could finally talk. Instead, when she got back to the library Ella was gone. Rapunzel had been deserted . . . again.

It didn't seem like Ella's style to just leave. All of her texts and scrolls were still on thc desk. But there was only one explanation for the way her friends had been acting. They weren't really her friends after all.

It hurt Rapunzel to think that Madame Gothel had been right all along. She hoped the old witch wouldn't rub it in too much. Because all she wanted right now was to be in her familiar room, under her rough sheet on her lumpy straw bed. She just wanted this awful day to come to an end.

Hand over hand, Rapunzel climbed up to her tower room. The dark clouds swirling overhead and rumbling thunder matched her mood. "Go ahead and flood," she said, scowling up at the sky. "I don't care if I ever make it back to Princess School."

Rapunzel's cheek was wet. She wiped the water drop away with her shoulder. It wasn't a tear. "I would never sob for that pack of pampered princesses," she mumbled. But as soon as she said it she felt closer to crying.

With a final heave Rapunzel lifted herself onto her windowsill and stopped dead.

"Surprise?" Snow said softly, her eyes wide. Behind her, Ella and Rose managed small apologetic smiles. Val looked scared enough to vomit.

"Surprise indeed!" Madame Gothel echoed. She spun around to face Rapunzel. Her mouth contorted into a sneer and her hands were on her hips.

Rapunzel had seen Madame Gothel angry before. That was no big shock. But what were all of her friends doing here — and who were those three princes tied up on the bed? Then, slowly, it began to dawn on her.

"You were throwing me a party?" she asked.

"A birthday party." Rose nodded.

"To make up for all the ones you missed," Val added.

"We wanted it to be a surprise, that's why —" Ella's voice dropped and disappeared as Madame Gothel raised her hands and turned to glare at her.

"Rats and bats!" the witch spat. "The final surprise is mine."

Madame Gothel's voice cracked. Her hands trembled and thunder shook the tower. Rapunzel pressed her back against the stone wall. Though she'd seen Madame Gothel mad before, she'd never seen her *this* mad.

"Your time with your friends has come to an end," Madame Gothel shrieked. She said the word *friends* like it burned her tongue. "In a few short moments they will be blind as bats, and your window will be permanently sealed!" The witch raised her arms to cast a spell.

The three princes on the bed struggled with their bindings. Rapunzel recognized them from the Coronation Ball. Oliver Eggert wore a look of determination. Allister Arlington looked mad. And poor handsome Hans Charming was there, too, hiding his face in his knees.

Dumbfounded, Rapunzel did nothing to stop Gothel's spell. She was too shocked to fight back.

"No!" Snow gasped.

"You can't!" Ella cried.

Rose locked arms with Val and moved with the other girls to block the tower's only opening. The princes struggled with their ties. Seeing her friends' courage, Rapunzel managed to take one step forward, then another.

"You can't keep me in forever," Rapunzel said quietly.

"You can't leave me," Madame Gothel choked out. Her hands were still held before her, but instead of looking like she was about to start casting she looked like she wanted to get them around Rapunzel's throat. "You can't leave me," she said again.

"I have been leaving you for years," Rapunzel retorted.

Madame Gothel's eyes flared, but Rapunzel thought she recognized something in them — something sad, like the way she had felt on the way home today. "But I always come back," she added more softly.

The room was suddenly silent except for the rain falling outside. Madame Gothel slowly let her hands fall to her sides. Rapunzel could hear her friends' cautious breathing. Nobody knew what was going to happen next.

"You always come back," Madame Gothel repeated. She looked from Rapunzel to the floor and back again.

"Lizard lips!" Madame Gothel cursed, stamping her narrow black boot on the floor and making the students jump. "I guess you do."

Rapunzel raised her eyebrows and cautiously tried

a half smile. The old witch actually seemed a little disappointed that she didn't have anything to be mad about.

"Of course I do." Rapunzel gestured around her tiny crowded room. "How could I give up all of this?"

Madame Gothel was caving. Rapunzel looked at her friends and winked. They were going to be okay! Snow was biting her ruby lips but managed to return her smile. Ella, Val, and Rose still looked a little nervous. And although Oliver and Allister had stopped struggling with their bindings, Hans still had his face hidden and was whimpering softly.

Madame Gothel seemed to be going over what Rapunzel had said again and again. Her leathery face had lost its cruel expression. Her shoulders drooped. She looked plain stumped.

Rapunzel felt her familiar confidence returning. She thumped Madame Gothel gently on the arm. "You know I don't have anyplace else to go," Rapunzel reminded her. "And besides," she admitted, "I kind of like it here."

# Chapter Twenty
# A Break in the Storm

Madame Gothel stood in a sort of stupor. For a few long moments she didn't move or say anything. Outside, the rain stopped. Everyone listened silently to the water dripping off the trees. They watched as the clouds blew quickly away to reveal an evening sky of deepest blue. On the horizon a band of dark orange was all that was left of the setting sun.

"I thought this was a party!" Rapunzel said, breaking the spell. She moved quickly to untie the three captive princes. Hans wiped his face and looked up sheepishly, obviously unaccustomed to being saved by a damsel.

"Oh, the food!" Snow leaned out the window. The cart of pies and cookies was just where Rose and Val had left it. "I hope it wasn't ruined by the rain!"

"Should we all go *down* now?" Val asked hopefully.

"I mean, it will be awfully hard to get all that food up here."

"I'll take care of it," Madame Gothel grumped, rousing from her stupor. Hans Charming retreated again to the bed as Madame Gothel advanced toward the window. She dropped the braided rope out the window and, after a quick wave of her wrist, the rope wrapped like a tentacle around the cart and lifted it to the level of Rapunzel's room.

"It's so soggy!" Snow said. With her hands on her cheeks, she surveyed her baked goods.

Madame Gothel mumbled something that sounded like "damp salamanders," waved her hands, and suddenly the cookies looked crisp and the pies' flaky crusts were restored.

"Oh, thank you!" Snow threw her arms around Madame Gothel. The witch cringed but Rapunzel noticed she didn't pull away.

When the cart was unloaded, everyone gathered around. Ella produced a candle stub from her pocket, poked it into the top of the biggest pie, and placed it in front of Rapunzel.

The candle mysteriously burst into flame and everyone, except Madame Gothel, who was blowing on her index finger, sang.

"Make a wish." Rose smiled.

Rapunzel closed her eyes and blew the candle out. When she opened them she looked around at her friends and her wicked foster mother. She couldn't remember the last time she'd felt so happy.

"What did you wish for?" Snow asked.

"Not telling." Rapunzel grinned.

As the food was served, the party guests relaxed more and more. Everything was delicious. Madame Gothel even tried the apple pie.

"Apple is my favorite," Snow said sweetly.

"Humph," Madame Gothel snorted with her mouth full. "I prefer bat wing stew," she announced as she shoveled in another bite of fruit and pastry.

The princes flocked around Rose. Hans fetched her a plate. Allister knelt beside her to hold her water glass and Oliver stared, starry-eyed, into her face. Rapunzel watched as Rose tried to brush them off like gnats. She was completely surrounded.

"So you were planning this all along?" Rapunzel asked Val. Val held a cookie in each hand.

"Mmm-hmm," he said with his mouth full.

Suddenly Rapunzel felt a bit foolish. Why would Rose try and steal her friend? She already had too many princes paying too close attention to her!

Ella sat beside Rapunzel on the bed and discreetly gestured toward Madame Gothel, who was lingering over her apple pie. "I still can't believe you made her mad enough to cause all of those storms!" she whispered.

"What?" Rapunzel asked.

"What?!" Madame Gothel roared, turning toward the girls.

"I didn't think you could hear. . . . I mean, it's just that Jezebel Jewelweed said . . . Well, I was only repeating —" Ella stammered.

"Spit it out," Madame Gothel said sternly, standing over poor Ella.

"She said the horrible weather could only be created by a powerful witch in danger of losing something she holds dear," Ella said quickly.

"Jezebel Jewelweed said that, did she?" Madame Gothel's mouth turned up into something like a smile. "Well, warts and warthogs. She used to be a pretty powerful witch herself until she took that desk job." Madame Gothel stood a little taller and smoothed the white streak in her hair.

"You did that?" Rapunzel asked. "I mean, all that weather was because of me?"

"You should be ashamed," Snow scolded, suddenly remembering that it was Madame Gothel who was responsible for most of the mess of the last week. "You mixed up all of our messages and the poor animals. They could have been really hurt!"

Madame Gothel turned to look at Snow. Snow took a step back and her voice got a little meeker. "I mean, it wasn't very nice," she finished.

"I mixed up the mail? And frightened the animals?" Madame Gothel laughed. It was practically a giggle. "I'm sorry," she said to Snow. But Rapunzel didn't think she seemed a bit remorseful. In fact she seemed a little proud. "I suppose I was angrier than I knew."

*And it was all over me,* Rapunzel marveled. She looked at Madame Gothel again and felt her own tug of pride. The old witch had quite a few surprises up her long sleeves.

The party lasted until the moon rose.

"I'd better go home," Ella said reluctantly as she stood to go. "It must be nearly midnight!"

Snow and Val left soon after Ella. "Many happy returns!" Val called when he reached the ground safely.

"Happily ever after!" Snow called before scampering into the woods.

Rose fought her way out of the circle of princes to give Rapunzel a quick hug. "We'll do it again next year." She smiled. "See you at school?" It was a question.

Rapunzel looked at Madame Gothel to see if she had heard. The witch was cleaning up the party mess, and at the mention of Princess School she began to bang things around a little harder.

"I hope so," Rapunzel said softly. Things had gone so well, but Madame Gothel's moods could change like, well, the weather.

Rose nodded her understanding and moved toward the window.

"Allow me!"

"No, me."

"Climb upon my back and I will carry you down." The princes began to vie for position to help Rose out the window and down thc side of the tower.

Rose winked at Rapunzel. "Back off, boys. I can do this myself." She slipped gracefully out and disappeared over the window ledge with a last wave.

"May I escort you home, Beauty?"

"Please, allow me?" The princes followed, still clamoring for Rose's attention.

Rapunzel watched them go, grinning. Poor Rose! She hoped she could lose them in the woods. If she couldn't they would probably spend the rest of the night serenading under her window!

Rapunzel grabbed the last empty plates and stacked them with the ones Madame Gothel had already cleared. Neither of them spoke, but the silence wasn't awkward, like it had been before. It felt comfortable.

"Mmm." Rapunzel licked a little berry pie filling off her thumb.

"You like that?" Madame Gothel asked. Her wild eyebrows almost met in the middle. "It's too sweet for me. But I might be able to make a pie for you once in a while."

"Thanks," Rapunzel answered. She was grateful. It would be nice to eat more than toadstools, eggs, and bitter greens. But another question hung in the air unanswered.

"So, uh, about Princess School," she started to ask.

"Oh, toads' tears," Madame Gothel cursed, sounding a little defeated and balling her hands into fists. "Just don't let them make you too royal!" she pouted.

Rapunzel laughed out loud. "Not a chance," she replied, looking straight at Madame Gothel. "Haven't you heard? My foster mother is a powerful witch." Rapunzel looked at Madame Gothel and smiled. Her birthday wish had just come true.

# There's more to Beauty than meets the eye.

Rose is tired of being called "Beauty" by her classmates, being smothered by her overprotective parents, and getting fussed over by her pesky guardian fairies. She wants to show the world she's more than just a pretty face—and she's forming a secret plan to do just that. But what if she goes too far?

SCHOLASTIC

www.scholastic.com/princessschool



PS4T